BLACK JACK

Terry Wright

2014, TWB Press
www.twbpress.com

Black Jack
Copyright © 2014 by Terry Wright

Cover Art by Terry Wright

ISBN: 978-1-936991-71-6

Acknowledgments

In the writing of this book, I've been blessed with the help of many writers and friends. I want to thank my wife first. Bobette has been my rock over the years, my biggest fan, my ideal reader, and my go-to gal when I need help with a character or a plot point. She's stood by me as I burned the midnight oil and pounded the keyboard until my fingers were numb. I love you.

Then there's the core of my RMFW critique group, Mario Acevedo (The Felix Gomez Vampire Detective Series), Jeanne Stein (The Anna Strong Vampire Bounty Hunter Series) and Warren Hammond (The KOP Series). I want to thank them for their professional insight and encouragement.

And last but not least, my fans, those of you who bought my books to help me support my writing habit. I owe you my sincerest gratitude forever.

Chapter One

IN MY TEN YEARS on the Denver police force, I never thought I'd set out to murder anyone. Yet here I sat in my unmarked squad car watching Martin Vallinski strut out of the donut shop at Sixth and Kalamath. My jaw muscles clenched. The bastard wasn't getting away. Not this time.

He wore a brown vest over a green flannel shirt, dirty denim jeans, and ragged tennis shoes. Scraggly brown hair hung over his forehead. Greasy skin, sharp cheekbones, and a piggy nose, his face was the last face Maria saw as she scratched it. He bore the scars on his cheek like a neon sign flashing: *GUILTY. GUILTY. GUILTY!*

Now my face would be the last face he'd ever see.

He killed my wife, god dammit!

Anger churned in my stomach like a twister on steroids. I wanted to spray his brains all over the donut shop window, but I had to grit my teeth to keep from losing my cool.

"Four-Adam-Nine. Meet the woman..."

I turned down the police radio chatter and watched him draw nearer, like a fly to a Venus Flytrap. Cops weren't supposed to kill the bad guys. We were supposed to arrest them. Bring them to justice, to a trial by a jury of their peers. But Vallinski was pond scum. He deserved to die.

Swaggering toward me like a punk from the hood, he pressed his left arm against his side, probably where he kept his gun, but I wasn't worried. I wore Kevlar under my pressed white shirt. The takedown would be clean: cuff him, drive him to the mountains, and put a bullet in his head. Too easy.

Would I get away with it? Who cared?

I climbed out of my car and beat a path toward him, gun drawn, and the black cloud of murder on my mind. My heart pounded a thousand jackhammers. I know. I know. *Thou shalt not kill.* It's written in the Book. *Revenge is mine sayeth the Lord,* but I'm thinking *an eye for an eye, a tooth for a tooth.*

Revenge is mine sayeth Jack Sabre.

"Vallinski!"

His eyes got big around. A curtain of fear dropped over his ugly mug.

"Get on the ground!"

He stopped, showed me his open hands. His wide eyes darted back and forth as if he expected a posse to surround him. But I was a one-man show.

My show. "You're under arrest." I had to make it look like a legitimate bust.

We weren't ten feet apart when a couple teenagers pushed out of the Dollar-A-Scoop Chinese restaurant and crossed between us, laughing and joking around. Just my luck to get a civilian or two killed in the crossfire. "Get out of the way!"

They stopped and locked eyes on my gun with that deer-in-the-headlights look.

"Move it!"

Vallinski lunged forward, shoved the couple into me, knocking all three of us to the ground.

The girl screamed. The boy cursed.

I pushed them off, hoping my gun wouldn't discharge in the scuffle. By the time I got to my feet, Vallinski had bolted across Kalamath. I ran after him, resisting the urge to shoot the bastard in the back. Too many people around.

Too many witnesses.

Reaching a Camry stopped at the red light on eastbound Sixth Avenue, he yanked open the driver door and pulled a screaming old woman out from behind the wheel. He threw her to the asphalt and jumped in. Add carjacking to the scumbag's rap sheet.

The Camry tore off through the red light and careened left, speeding head-on into southbound Kalamath traffic. The bottom dropped out of my stomach. He was getting away. Again.

Fighting a hot wave of panic, I ran to my squad car. Now I had to chase him. The captain would be on my ass like slippery on oil, but I wasn't about to let Vallinski escape.

Hitting the grill blue lights and siren, I peeled out after him, against the flow of traffic, against a red light. Oncoming cars skidded and spun out. Weaving through the mayhem, I wished

I'd taken time to buckle up.

Vallinski whipped a u-turn and raced west on the Sixth Avenue freeway.

I cranked my steering wheel, dodged a pickup, fishtailed wildly, and accelerated after the Camry.

Keying the radio mike, "One-Adam-Eight, hot pursuit, westbound Sixth Avenue." All chases had to be called in. Dispatch would notify the captain. He'd decide how the pursuit was handled...or terminated. I was a good cop. I followed the rules. Until now. "Tell the captain I found Vallinski."

The Camry was no match for my car. Within seconds, I was riding the rear bumper, so close I could see Vallinski's bugged-out eyeballs in his rearview mirror. Bet he thought the devil was on his tail.

We cut through traffic like NASCAR drivers tearing up the track. The siren made my nerves crawl. My throat felt clamped in a Hulk Hogan chokehold. But I could handle the pain. I was pissed.

"One-Adam-Eight."

The gravelly voice on the radio belonged to

Captain Salvador. My stomach knotted. How was I going to explain a high-speed pursuit with Martin Vallinski?

"One-Adam-Eight," the captain shouted.

He'd ordered me to stay away from this case.

"Jack! What are you doing?"

I was too emotionally involved.

"Jack?"

Damn right I was. I'd lost everything that mattered most to me. My love. My life. My future. Hot tears stung my eyes. "I'll get him, captain."

Veering right, Vallinski swung around a bread truck. I went left, blasted past the truck and swerved in behind the Camry again, close and tight, now screaming over the bridge at Sheridan.

"I told you to let the task force handle Vallinski."

"They haven't done squat," I shouted into my radio. "Not enough evidence. What kind of excuse is that? It's been six months."

"Jack. I'm on your side."

"Then let me do my job."

"It's not going to bring Maria back."

"This isn't about her. It's about me." It was

about revenge. Doling out justice where justice was due. Murdering a murderer.

"Come in here. We'll talk about it."

The Camry sideswiped an SUV in the left lane. Sparks flew like welding flack. "Damn!" I was forced to back off the throttle, tap the brakes. Hulk Hogan tightened his stranglehold.

Tires smoking, the SUV swerved right just in time to let me squeeze by the crash wall. In this race from hell there'd be no yellow flags, no pit stops. This was Jack Sabre NASCAR. All out to the end. One winner. One loser.

I stomped on the gas.

The radio clicked. "Stop, Jack. That's an order."

"You should back me up on this."

"I'll have your badge."

My insides shuddered. Salvador loved Maria too. He wanted her killer apprehended just as much as I did. But his threat didn't deserve an answer, even if he was my father-in-law.

"Let the Lakewood boys take it from here."

The Wadsworth exit flew by. Two Lakewood cruisers screamed up the onramp and fell in behind me. Glory hogs, joining the excitement. A cop's job was normally mundane, 99 percent boring, 1 percent terror. This chase would make their day, but putting Vallinski on a slab was going to make mine.

"Back off, Jack!"

In the left lane, a minivan must've been doing 40 miles an hour. Brake lights blinked. The driver was probably freaking out over all the flashing lights coming up fast from behind. His right turn signal winked on. At a hundred miles an hour, none of us in this life or death chase had time for proper driving etiquette.

Vallinski veered right to get around the minivan.

The minivan switched lanes to the right.

Brakes screamed.

I heard the crash, even over the wail of my siren. The Camry smacked the van in its right rear quarter panel, knocking it into a sideways skid. A perfect PIT maneuver, but the Camry's hood flew over the roof, came spinning at my car like a giant Frisbee.

"Shit!" I ducked. The flyaway hood raked my roof and bounced off the asphalt behind me. The glory hogs' tires screamed. Metal crunched.

The minivan flipped and rolled, throwing parts like a Kansas tornado. Hulk Hogan slammed me to the mat. I couldn't breathe. No one could survive a wreck that horrendous. I hit my brakes, thinking to stop and help the victims, but the Camry took off like the Batmobile. I clenched my teeth, got off the brakes, mashed the gas. Back in the chase.

Smoke billowed from the Camry. In minutes, the engine would be scrap-metal. Hunched over the steering wheel, Vallinski looked like he was driving the car forward on sheer will alone. But my front bumper was on his ass. I had him now.

A quick glance in my rearview told me the Lakewood cops had dropped out to assist at the accident scene.

Vallinski was all mine.

The captain's voice came over the radio. "Jack. I want to see you in my office. Now!"

"I've almost got him, sir."

"Jack. You heard me."

"I've got him! I've got him!"

"It's Lakewood's jurisdiction!"

"It's *my* bust, god dammit!"

"Get back here! That's an order."

Fuck him.

My palms sweated. This chase had to end. I rammed the Camry's rear bumper and bulldozed the car onto the shoulder. In a cloud of dirt, the Camry flipped and landed upside down next to a barbwire fence, wheels spinning.

I slammed on the brakes.

Beyond the fence lay a stretch of open field that ended at a car dealership. A million acres of inventory sparkled under the Colorado sun. In a maze like that, he'd be as hard to find as Alice's rabbit in Wonderland.

I pinched the radio mike. "10-50. He crashed at Indiana. I've got him."

"Lakewood backup is on the way."

Vallinski crawled out the driver door window. His hair was a mop. Blood ran down his cheek from a gash in his head. He may have survived the crash, but he wasn't going to survive me.

"Foot pursuit," I radioed, drew my gun, and threw open the car door.

"Stand down," the captain's voice shouted back.

The killer tried to squeeze between two strands of barbwire, knees and elbows pumping hard, but his vest caught on the barbs and snared him. He thrashed about like a trapped rat.

"Jack! You hear me? Don't do anything stupid."

Elbows locked and braced on the hood, I held my gun in both hands, a Glock 22 .40 caliber light-weight killing machine, pointed at the squirreling murderer. I had Maria's killer lined up in my sights, not twenty feet away. My finger tightened on the trigger. I hoped my hammering heartbeat wouldn't screw up my aim.

Sirens approached in the distance.

I felt a tingle in my shoulder, electric as Maria's touch, as if she were standing beside me, a coconspirator in my act of revenge.

The sensation gave me pause.

Reality sank in.

Though I had every right to kill her murderer, how could I do anything so cold-blooded? Shoot him down like a rabid dog. Had losing Maria taken my soul? This one act of revenge would certainly ruin my career and destroy whatever future I had left. I'd probably never get out of jail. Freedom from this constant gnaw of anger in my guts wouldn't be worth the price of my freedom. Sweat leaked into my right eye, blurring my aim. I had to admit, when it came down to pulling the trigger, I couldn't do it.

"Fuck!"

I loosened my finger on the trigger. "Vallinski! Show me your hands. You're under arrest for the murder of Maria Sabre."

As if divine intervention had intentions of its own, Vallinski pulled a gun. His hand shook as he took aim at me.

"Drop your weapon." I doubted he could even hit my car.

Two shots. *Pop, pop.* One bullet spider-webbed my windshield; the other thunked into my radiator. A plume of billowing steam hissed up in front of me. I didn't know whether to shit in my pants or sing hallelujah! The dumbass just gave me a reason to shoot him. No killing could be more justified than self-defense.

"This one's for you, Maria," I whispered and pumped the trigger twice...

Bang! Bang!

...like cops are taught to shoot, two shots at

a time in quick succession, until the threat is stopped.

> *Bang! Bang!*
>
> Vallinski slumped over.
>
> My ears rang.
>
> I smiled.
>
> They didn't call me Black Jack for nothing.

Chapter Two

THE WAITING AREA outside Captain Salvador's office smelled like dirty socks. It was a narrow room with one window, like an execution chamber. I sat in a cushy chair, minor ass comfort before the major ass chewing that awaited me.

On the table, magazines lay fanned out. *Police Shooter. Guns R Us.* I was tempted to pick one up, but I didn't want anything to distract me from the warm glow I felt inside knowing Vallinski got what he was due.

Two uniformed officers walked by the window, glanced in and looked away quickly, as if the sight of me hurt their eyes.

Screw 'em.

What the hell did they know? They still had their wives at home. Their lives weren't shattered. They weren't condemned to a lonely, miserable existence. They weren't missing Maria and cursing God for taking her away.

I did the right thing, damn it.

Vallinski had a gun. Justifiable use of deadly force. I was sure the captain would see it my way.

Miss Mina Finetree, the captain's receptionist, opened the door. She wore her hair up in a brown grandma bun, black rimmed glasses thick as submarine windows, and a white-collared shirt buttoned up to her eyebrows. "He'll see you now."

I got out of the chair, swallowed hard, and scooted past her. She kept her distance like I had leprosy, but even this close I found her perfume delicious. Miss goody-two-shoes had a wilder side.

Stepping into the captain's office, my heart thumped my ribcage. He wasn't alone. Three stern faces turned my direction. I got a creepy feeling that these men hadn't come here to congratulate me for a job well done.

Benny Peterson stood beside the desk, feet apart and arms crossed over his chest like Superman dressed in a cheap K-Mart suit. He was the tall, narrow-faced detective who'd dragged his feet in Maria's murder investigation. The way he glared at me, I thought his bug-eyes would pop out and bounce on the floor.

Standing next to him, a fat, balding man held a folder open in his upturned hands, much like a preacher holding a Bible. He looked at me and then glanced at Captain Salvador sitting in the high-back leather chair behind his desk. The dead-serious look in his eyes alarmed me. His thick black mustache couldn't hide his pursed lips.

"Jack Sabre," the captain said. "Have a seat."

I didn't find the formal tone in his voice welcoming. "No thanks, I'll stand." And keep the high ground so I didn't have to look up at these clowns.

Finetree closed the door behind me. I suddenly felt the walls close in. Anxiety itched under my Kevlar vest.

"You know Detective Peterson."

I wanted to sneer at the foot-dragger but kept my cop face on and moved to the front of Salvador's desk.

"District Attorney Daryl Dodson." He

indicated the fat man.

I didn't look at him. "Do we really have to go through all this, sir?"

"You screwed up, Jack."

I looked the captain straight in the eye. "I got Vallinski. That's all that matters."

Salvador stood, extended his right hand, palm up. "Your badge. Give it here."

My heart seized. "What?"

"I warned you, Jack."

"He was getting away, damn it."

Detective Peterson chimed in. "You disobeyed a direct order and continued the pursuit."

Captain Salvador shot the detective an iron look. "I'll handle this."

"It was my case," Peterson shouted.

I wanted to punch him. "And you sat on it. You didn't—"

"Enough!" Salvador waggled his upturned fingers. "Your badge, Jack. Hand it over."

My face felt numb. "So that's it? Just like that. I'm on your shit list?"

"You're on administrative leave with pay. That's the good news."

I caught the smug look on Peterson's face, wanted to wipe it off with the butt of my gun. But I didn't have a gun. Earlier, I had to turn it over to the Internal Affairs Shoot Team. "What's the bad news?"

The fat DA spoke. "This is the Shoot Team's report." He waved the file. "I'm taking it to the grand jury. If I get my way, it'll be Murder One for you."

My legs felt like liquorish sticks. "No way!" I held up my hands, took a step back. "Vallinski had a gun. It was self defense."

"Doesn't matter," Salvador said with his hand still extended. "You shouldn't have initiated the chase."

"But he carjacked an old lady."

"Only because you stalked him," Peterson said.

"Stalked?" I glared at the detective. "It was a stakeout."

"An unauthorized stakeout," the captain said.

"There's a rule of law here," DA Dodson put in. "*Ex turpi causa*. From your dishonorable cause, Vallinski acted dishonorably. It's your fault for what happened."

"You've got to be shittin' me."

"You should've kept your nose out of my case." Peterson spat out the words.

"Come on, Jack," Salvador said. "Give me your badge."

I looked at his face, remembered the pride that shown in his eyes the day he gave me Maria's hand at the altar. Now I saw disdain. We were family, damn it. His daughter was dead. He had no call to treat me like a criminal.

"The badge!"

My neck hairs prickled. "All right! You want it..." I unclipped the badge from my belt. "You got it," and flipped it like a quarter onto his desktop. "Satisfied?"

"And your ID card."

Hot anger seared my veins. I jerked out my wallet and pulled the ID card from its window flap. *Detective Jack Sabre* it read, superimposed over the blue outline of a police badge. *#181248.* My mug shot took up half the card: buzz-cut hair, hard cheekbones, serious lips. I was all business the day I made detective. Two years ago. I slapped the card on the desk.

"And the keys to the squad car."

"You want my liver too?"

"If it belongs to the department, then yes."

Digging the keys out of my pocket: "This is the thanks I get for catching a killer." I slammed them on the desk.

"Therein lies the problem." The DA closed his folder.

I glanced back and forth between the three men, felt like a train was coming at me head-on. "What problem?"

Peterson dropped his Superman stance and stepped toward me. "Vallinski didn't kill Maria."

A burning sensation crept up my backbone. "Yes he did."

"Sorry, Jack," Salvador said. "His DNA didn't match the evidence at the crime scene."

"The skin under her fingernails belongs to someone else," Peterson added.

The wind leaked out of my lungs. "Why didn't you tell me?"

"It wasn't your case."

I looked at the captain, hoping he would say something that would get my neck out of this noose. "If not Vallinski, then who?"

"We don't know."

"You killed an innocent man," Peterson said.

"Innocent?" I felt dizzy. "The scumbag carjacked an old lady, broke a million traffic laws, hit and run, drew a gun on me, shot up my car—"

"He was no saint," Salvador cut in. "We could wallpaper the shitter with his rap sheet. But we've already eliminated him as a suspect."

DA Dodson moved to the door. "I'll be seeing you, Jack, after the grand jury convenes." He left the room, taking the air with him.

I couldn't breathe. That warm feeling I'd felt earlier turned arctic. Maria's killer was still out there. I glanced at my badge on the desktop; it felt as far away as Saturn. "Please, Captain—"

"Go home, Jack." His tone sounded final. "Get a lawyer."

"You can't shut me out. Not now."

"I already have." He returned to his seat and stared at me.

I was screwed. I looked at Benny Peterson. "You should've told me."

His eyes narrowed. "You're going down hard, Jack."

"Fuck you." I stormed to the door. "I don't need you sons of bitches or that badge to find Maria's killer."

"Let it go, Jack," Salvador barked.

Fists clenched, I charged out the door and through the waiting room.

Peterson's footsteps clomped behind me. "What happened to you, Jack? You used to be a nice guy. Now you're an asshole."

I held my breath and reigned in the urge to turn around and deck him.

Mina Finetree looked up from her reception desk. "Sorry, Jack."

"Yeah. Sucks to be me." On my way out, I slammed the door.

In the hallway, a woman's mournful cries echoed off the walls, coming from the chief's office. Several officers and precinct staffers had gathered in the hall. I pushed past them to the window and looked in. An old woman wearing a tattered green dress and a ratty blue sweater sat in front of the chief's desk, sobbing into a tissue.

"Vallinski's mother," Peterson said from behind me.

"I know." I recalled our conversation that

morning.

"What's he done now?" she'd asked me through the screen door on her front porch.

"Just a few questions," I'd said.

"He went to the donut shop on Kalamath."

"Why?"

"Somebody owed him money."

The rest was history. Now, a million years later, she looked up, dabbing her nose with the tissue. Tears streaked her blotchy complexion. Her eyes met mine through the glass. A glint of recognition then red-eyed rage. "He did it," she shouted, pointing at me with a shaky finger. "He killed my boy!"

I felt gut punched.

Chapter Three

THE STAR BAR STOOD as a relic to downtown Denver's skid-row days. It was barely wider than a phone booth, dark and dank. I walked in on threadbare carpet, passed a scarred pool table, and inhaled the stink of stale beer and vomit. Stick furniture took up most of the floor space, pale tables and chairs made of pine that would break up real easy in a bar fight. Tattered nineteenth century wallpaper wept from the walls. A long bar occupied the right wall, fronted by wooden stools and backed by a large mirror with a circle-star engraved in the glass. Shelves crammed with booze bottles, stacked CD jewel cases, a grungy microwave and brown-stained Mr. Coffee, and more clutter than I could shake a gun at, gave the place a homey, junkyard appeal.

A sign read: *Draft Beer – 2 bucks.*

I was thirsty for something stronger.

To its loyal patrons, this dive was known as a *Number One Bar*. The toilet didn't work. We had to go out in the alley to pee. There was nowhere to go number two.

My entrance drew glares from a couple of red-nosed drunks sitting at the bar, skinny bums with weathered faces, wiry hair, and rags for clothes. "Uh-oh!" one quipped to the other. "It's that detective."

Ex-detective. That reality made my stomach turn over.

They raised their hands in mock surrender. "Don't shoot, off-licer."

Smartasses. If they wanted to piss me off, this was an especially good day to do it.

"Shut up, Danny," the bartender said, closing the cash drawer. The round-bellied Mexican with Elvis sideburns wore a brown vest over a white t-shirt and a flower-print apron. Everyone called him Porky. "You and that idiot friend of yours better behave." He looked at me. "Pay 'em no mind, Jack."

I took his advice and moved to the bar. "The usual."

"You're early."

He killed my boy.

"I had a bad day." Feeling pistol-whipped, I sat on my favorite cracked vinyl barstool and set my elbows on a bar-top etched with deep black gouges of graffiti. One was my doing: *MARIA*. I'd carved the A's as upside-down hearts and crossed them with little arrows. My soul ached. This was hallowed ground.

"Every day's a bad day for you, Jack." Porky set a water-spotted glass in front of me, poured two fingers of Old Crow from the bottle, started to take it away.

I grabbed his arm. "Leave it."

"This ain't gonna bring her back..." His brown-eyed gaze zeroed in on my face as if he'd seen some kind of ugly growth on my nose. "What happened?"

Was my defrocking that obvious? "The captain and I had a little misunderstanding." I picked up the glass and knocked back a fiery mouthful of liquid relief. "Went in for an ass chewing, came out with an assendectomy."

"You write a bad ticket?"

He killed my boy!

"Something like that."

Porky leaned on the bar, his fat face so close the smell of tobacco tainted his words. "Ya gotta learn to stay out of trouble, Jack." He poured another two fingers. "Si?"

The last thing I needed was a lecture. "You've got customers to take care of." I cocked my head at the drunks and downed the two fingers.

"Go easy on this stuff." He set the bottle in front of me.

"Yeah." I snatched up the bottle. What did he know? I'd set out to murder a scumbag and ended up killing him in self defense. It was a turn of events in my favor...or so I'd thought. *Ex turpi causa*, my ass.

Now I was the bad guy.

He killed my boy!

And Maria's killer was still walking around breathing good people's air. I deserved to get bombed. I refilled my glass.

One of the drunks cackled. "No drinkin' on duty, off-licer."

"Go fuck yourself."

Porky moved to the two drunks. "You boys

better chill."

Holding the glass to my mouth like the barrel of a cocked gun, I stroked Maria's carved name with my fingertip. Tears stung my eyes. I knocked back the Old Crow. Whiskey's hot breath awakened memories that were better left sleeping:

***

A hot summer afternoon. Thunderstorms brewed over Denver. At Colorado Boulevard and Colfax Avenue, the signal lights were on the blink. I stood in the middle of the intersection directing traffic. It felt more like wading in a pool of mechanical sharks. Quick feet were my only defense.

I blew my whistle at a white Toyota coupe stopped in the left turn lane and holding up rush-hour traffic to westbound Colfax. The driver, a woman with long hair, probably couldn't hear my whistle over all the horns honking around her.

"Come on, lady!" I waved her through, but she just sat there. I glanced up to ask God, "why me?" and noticed a squall line pounding downtown. If I didn't get this traffic unsnarled soon, I was going to get soaked.

Blowing my whistle, I got everybody stopped in all directions and stomped toward the Toyota. I heard the starter cranking. She was pumping the gas so hard the car rocked on its springs.

The engine had to be as flooded as the Titanic.

I made it to her open window. "Lady! You're going to kill the battery."

"It won't start," she shouted as if I hadn't figured that out by myself. She kept cranking and pumping.

Horns honked as if that alone would solve the problem.

"You flooded it!"

Letting go of the key, she threw herself into the seatback, gripped the steering wheel with both hands and groaned. "My mechanic said he fixed it."

Thunder rumbled in the distance.

***

I swallowed another belt of Old Crow.

"Have some coffee, Jack," Porky said.

My eyes focused on him standing in front

of me with a mug in his hand. I waved it off. "Maria was my second wife, you know."

"Not this again—"

"Her name was Karen...my first wife...Karen."

He leaned on the bar. "Go home, Jack."

I felt dizzy as a windmill in a hurricane. "When we got married, I was a mechanic, busted a few knuckles, made a few bucks, drank a few beers. My contribution to the world: a tune up and an oil change."

"Give yourself a break."

"Not very rewarding...or memorable. I was destined to die with a fuckin' wrench in my hand."

"The whiskey's talkin' again, Jack." He grasped the bottle from the bar. "Makes you a whiner."

I grabbed the bottle neck. "So I became a cop."

Porky let go of the bottle. "Stop feelin' sorry for yourself. It's not like you—"

"Figured I'd make a difference, make my life matter, but Karen hated...Karen hated being a cop's wife. 'Is this the day you come home in a box, buster?' Buster. I hated it when she called me buster. Damn drama queen."

"You can't blame her. Police work is dangerous."

"Yeah, I could get my finger slammed in a car door."

"Maybe she cared, that's all."

"She left!" I freshened my drink and gulped it down. "Maria treated me right...now she's gone."

"Life ain't always about happily ever after. It's what you do next that counts. What are you gonna do next, Jack, drink yourself to death?"

"I'm gonna find her killer." I poured more Old Crow, slopping some on the bar. "Get my badge back."

"You got canned?" Porky scratched his bushy sideburns. "Must've been some fucked up ticket."

"I'll get my badge back."

"When, Jack? After this drink or the next one?"

"You'll see."

One of the drunks called out, "Another round over here, ya fuckin' wetback."

Porky straightened. "I'm gonna toss them loudmouths out on their ears."

"Customers," I said. "Be nice to the customers."

He flipped me off. "I'll remember you said that. Someday you'll be one of them bums." Then he shouted to the drunks. "Remember the Alamo, you Yankee gringos."

I gazed into my glass of booze. Three short years ago, I was light years from this barstool:

***

Leaning toward the woman driver, I was about to say something stupid like "you're holding up traffic," as if she didn't know that, when I saw her face. Her dark brows were tight lines of frustration, her cheeks smooth, a perfect slant to her nose, and her lips full and kissable red. If my eyes were sponges they couldn't have soaked up enough of her beauty.

Horns blasted me back to the problem at hand. I looked around at a sea of car roofs radiating heat. What a mess. The thunderstorm loomed closer. Dark clouds were about to blot out the sun. I decided to call for backup and keyed the radio mike on my collar. "Two-Adam-Four, dispatch."

As I awaited the reply, the woman cranked her body around and looked out the back window. Brown hair tumbled over her bare shoulder, her olive-skinned bare shoulder, a shoulder I wanted to touch, to kiss. My eyes wandered to her blouse. The low-cut smile of lace revealed a tantalizing slope of plump cleavage. I imagined my face buried between those two lovely...

She looked up at me. I blinked and shifted my eyes so I wouldn't get caught gawking.

"Please call my father," she said, her voice smooth as Beethoven.

Her father would kill me for what I was thinking. "Daddy didn't buy you a cell phone?"

"Battery's dead." She held it out to me like I'd check it for myself.

My radio squelched. "Dispatch, Two-Adam-Four, go ahead."

"10-43. I need assistance with traffic."

"Standby."

Clouds covered the sun and cooled the air. "Does your father own a tow truck?"

Terry Wright

"He's captain at District Four."

Salvador's daughter. Maria. I'd heard she wore a chastity belt with bear trap jaws.

Her pleading brown eyes searched my face, but one eye didn't move, the right one, like it was made of glass. Spooked the hell out of me. I imagined her eye watching us bang from the bottom of a water glass on the nightstand. Gave me the willies.

"Call him on your radio."

She intrigued me. A woman who'd grown up in a cop's family. Maybe she understood the sacrifices of law enforcement. Things might work out between us. Unlike Karen...

But that eye—

"Please," she cooed.

The wind came up, kicking dust in my face.

Dispatch said, "Two-Adam-Four. Adam-Seven is responding."

"10-4." That would be Chad Brendon. A good ol' boy.

Thunder boomed.

Chad was on the way, but I still had to get the Toyota moving. I didn't need her father's help for that.

I stooped to the window but kept my distance from *the eye*. "Put your foot all the way down on the gas pedal, hold it to the floor, and turn the key."

"It won't start."

"Trust me, I used to be a mechanic." Boy, did that sound like an oxymoron: *trust* and *mechanic* in the same sentence. "In a past life," I added to distance myself from a bad rap.

She floored the gas and turned the key. The engine sputtered a few times, then more and more until it finally caught and wound up. A cloud of black smoke spewed from the tailpipe.

"Yes!" She smiled. "Thank you, officer...officer...?"

"Sabre, Jack Sabre, ma'am."

"You're a nice guy, Jack."

I touched the bill of my cap, backed away, and waved her through the intersection. As the one-eyed beauty drove off, I wished I'd gotten her phone number.

The rain came down like Niagara Falls on a floating barrel.

***

Swallowing whiskey, I savored the burn in my throat. Yeah, I was a nice guy. Back then.

He killed my boy!

Now I was a murderer. I could live with that knowing Vallinski killed Maria. But now—

Old Crow swirled into my glass. I wasn't so drunk that I didn't realize I hadn't poured it myself.

Slender fingers gripped my bottle. Red fingernails. Long. Curved. Sexy. The kind of fingernails I'd love to have scratching my back. Pulse on rapid fire, my gaze traversed up a slender arm, slipped over smooth white skin, climbed to a round shoulder, sleek neck, and blonde hair framing a soft face with cherry lips and blueberry eyes.

I'd twisted around so far to take in the view that I wobbled on my barstool, breaking the trance and slamming me back to the moment. The hooker had a lot of nerve crashing my pity party. "Where the fuck did you come from?"

"Share?" She held up the bottle.

I grabbed it away from her. "I drink alone." The bottle went under my arm protectively. "Beat it!"

She sat on the next barstool. "I know what happened."

"Shit happened!"

"I know something else about you."

What could this hooker know about me? Other than the fact I was smashed. No-brainer there. I looked her up and down. Red high heels, black nylons, sharp knees, short skirt hiked up to her stocking straps. I checked the undone buttons on her white blouse, the wide gap of cleavage—

"Hey, b-baby." Danny the drunk had staggered up to her. "How 'bout we have us a little party? I'll bring the booze, you bring the pussy."

"Buzz off, numb nuts," she said.

Her tart response got a rise out of my eyebrows. This whore was no pushover.

The other drunk, still sitting at the bar, laughed. "You gonna take that from a bitch!"

I didn't see Porky, figured he must have gone out back to take a whiz.

Danny snorted. "Don't be shy, darlin'. Gimme some lovin'." He looped his grubby arm around her shoulders and yanked her body against his.

She shoved him back.

I was all right with the razzing. The boys were just having fun. But no touching. No sexual assaulting. In my sloshed mind, I was still a cop. My temper jumped to hyper-drive. "Hey, shit-for-brains, keep your greasy mitts off her!"

He grinned a toothless grin. "I found her first." He lunged at her again. "Come on, baby."

"You stupid fuck!" I yanked the bottle from under my arm, jumped up, and bashed the bum over the head. He went down like the Bismarck.

I glanced at the bottle, surprised I'd hit him with it and surprised it didn't break. Guess that only happened in the movies.

His buddy crawled up, started pawing on him. "Danny. Danny." He shook him and looked up, white-faced. "He's dead. Ya kilt him."

Two dead scumbags in one day? Not bad. May as well make it three. "You're next." I reared back with the bottle, and teetering on alcohol-wobbly legs, I had to brace myself on the barstool to keep from falling on my ass. Never mind the Old Crow that drained down my shirtsleeve.

"Go easy, Jack," the woman said behind me. I looked back, amazed that I'd put myself between her and the drunk. Serve and protect, that was Jack Sabre, with or without a badge.

Smiling, she propped one elbow on the bar and crossed her slender legs. A high heel dangled from her upturned toes. My mouth watered. Whatever she charged, she was damn well worth it.

"What the hell's goin' on in here?" Porky shouted from the back door and charged in.

I lowered the drained bottle and set it on the bar. Alcohol vapor oozed from my shirtsleeve and stung my eyes. The adrenaline rush dwindled to hot ash in my stomach.

"He kilt Danny," the drunk cried out, holding the unconscious man's scruffy head in his lap.

Waddling toward us, Porky shot me a what-the-fuck look. "I can't leave you alone for one minute!"

"He st...started it." My tongue felt like a pretzel.

"You're cut off, Jack."

I sat on my barstool, my oasis in a sea of misery.

The hooker touched my shoulder.

"Thanks."

"No sweat."

Porky kneeled to the downed bum. "He's just out cold."

"Damn!" I crowed. "I should'a hit him harder."

"You're an asshole, Jack."

I shrugged. "So I've heard." Sticks and stones.

Porky stood. "And you." He pointed to the sleaze sitting next to me. "Get out of my bar."

My boozed up ego took offense to that. I'd saved her from a mauling. She owed me a drink. "Come on, Porky."

"Whores are trouble." He gestured to the drunks on the floor as evidence. "She's eighty-sixed."

I spoke without thinking. "She goes. I go."

Porky bobbed his head. "I'm good with that."

Danny moaned.

The other drunk helped get him to his feet and back up on his barstool. Porky checked the lump on the side of the idiot's head. "That's gotta hurt like hell." Then he turned to me. "I thought you were leaving."

I touched *MARIA*'s name I'd carved in the bar. I didn't want to leave her, leave hallowed ground, leave my self-pity—

"Don't make me call a real cop," Porky said.

"Fuck you!"

The whore stood and adjusted her skirt to a less revealing level. "I'll give you a ride, Jack."

Whoa there, baby. I wasn't going anywhere with this hooker. I didn't even know her name. Did I look like a chump?

She pulled a folded bill from her bra and dropped it on the bar. "For your trouble," she told Porky.

A C note! What the hell kind of whore would pay my tab and tip like Donald Trump?

My brain started firing questions Tommy gun style. Who was she? Why did she come here? What did she know? To find the answers, I'd have to accept her offer for a ride.

She helped me off the barstool, took my arm, and guided me toward the door.

Damn! I suddenly had to go number one.

Chapter Four

OUTSIDE THE STAR BAR, the air smelled like exhaust and carried the ever-present drone of traffic. The hooker lugged me to her car, a silver Mercedes sedan with windows tinted so dark that if I were still a cop I'd write her a ticket. She propped my drunk ass against the fender and used a keyless remote to unlock the doors. I noticed the parking meter at her front bumper flashed red. *EXPIRED*. Damn hooker had no respect for the law. Imagine that. A legal-minded hooker. I laughed.

"What's so funny?"

"A private joke. Nothin'."

"Ha. Ha."

I looked up and took a deep breath, trying to focus my eyes. The sky was dark gray, and streetlights winked on. I wished it was tomorrow.

She dunked me into the passenger seat. My bladder felt like it was going to pop. The door slammed. Groping for the seatbelt, I hoped I wouldn't piss all over her leather upholstery.

She slid in behind the wheel. Her short dress hiked up far enough to expose the white of her thighs above her stockings. That male-instinctive yank of desire made me feel as if I'd just cheated on Maria. I shifted my gaze out the windshield.

The Mercedes peeled away from the curb at whip-lash speed. My bladder seized. "Slow down, damn it!"

She careened the car onto northbound Speer. "What's the matter with you, Jack, hanging out in a dive like that?"

I wanted to say the Star outclassed her pricey ass, remind her she wasn't welcome there, but considering her clothes, the C-note in her bra, and this Mercedes, I decided to tell her the truth. "I go there to do my serious drinking."

"There are better places, with music and food, women and dancing. Nice places Maria would approve of."

"Maria?" This took too much thinking for

so much booze. My wife knew the hooker? "How did you know Maria?"

"She'd want you to go someplace fun."

"I don't drink for fun." My toasted brain had jumped from the hooker knowing Maria to defending my drinking. Drunks did that a lot. "Drinking is hard work. Heartbreaking work."

She'd gotten me on this roll; she'd better hear me out.

"I drink to remember every hair on her head, every word she ever uttered, every scent from every inch of her body, the softness of every curve and the tenderness of her touch. The Star is a drinking bar. Anything else would be a distraction." I shot her a disapproving glare. "Like you."

She stopped at a red light. "You're better than that."

What did she know? "Who the hell are you, anyway?"

"Let's just say we have a mutual friend."

"That explains everything. Fuck you both." Right about then I'd have been happy to take a whizz on her seat.

She took a right. "He tells me you're going

to investigate Maria's murder on your own."

My pickled brain tried to remember who knew I'd said that. Captain Salvador. Puke-for-brains Peterson. Maybe busybody Finetree had overheard. "Where are you taking me?"

"He wants to talk to you."

"He who?"

"You'll see."

The Mercedes turned left into the railroad yard, and the luxury ride became a bladder-punisher. Plunging through a bright beam of light, the car thudded over tracks, skidded right, and passed by a lumbering diesel locomotive. Train brakes squealed. Couplers slammed together. Compressed air hissed. The sudden blast of an air horn nearly startled the piss out of me, literally.

I scrunched down in the seat, knees pressed together like a Catholic school girl.

The hooker stopped her car next to a black Lincoln. Its headlights were off, just the park lights were on, and no dome light came on when the doors opened. I could barely make out two silhouettes approaching the Mercedes' illegally tinted passenger window. They looked like the Michelin Man and his taller brother Sasquatch. My stomach rolled over. Big guys meant big trouble. "Look, Lady, we gotta get out of here."

She scowled at me as if I was the damn drama queen of the Union Pacific.

The men were getting closer.

"Go, go! Dammit. Go!"

"Just talk to him."

"Him. There's two of them. Who are they?"

My door flew open. The dome light blinded me. Burly hands grabbed my arm, yanked me out, and flung me to the ground. Gravel grated my face to road rash. I inhaled the stench of oil and diesel, saw the hazy form of a boxcar and both goons looming over me. They were dressed in black, ski masks and all.

"What the fuck?"

A boot kicked me in the ribcage, knocked the wind out of my lungs. Gasping, I rolled over, got kicked again, in the kidney. Hot urine blossomed in my pants.

The hooker had lied. These guys didn't want to talk. The sons of bitches wanted to kill me.

"Stop it!" the whore shouted. She'd gotten out of the car and was tugging on the tall goon's arm, Sasquatch. "You said you weren't going to hurt him."

"I lied."

Michelin Man kicked me again. In the head.

Stars. Spinning.

Sasquatch bent to my ear. "Keep your nose out of our business," he growled.

More stars. The coppery taste of blood.

"Or you'll find yourself tits up like your wife."

I was going out for the count, but not before I recognized the bastard's voice.

Chapter Five

I REGAINED CONSCIOUSNESS under a boxcar, between the rails, curled in a tight ball. Blinking crud out of my eyes, I swallowed bile and wondered how the hell I got here, but my mind was a blank sheet of paper. Black paper. Another wonderful, fun-filled night of drinking I'd never remember.

My guts clenched, and I puked. I'd heard someone say that a man's life flashed behind his eyelids when he died. I should've been so lucky.

No childhood memories of my mom and dad, just vomit pooling in oily gravel at my face. No cinematic replay of my high school friends cheering me on during the big game. I heaved.

Touch-down.

I spit. My fat lip felt Texan. I tried to move, but my ribs were shark jaws in my chest. A jackhammer started jacking into my skull. My molars hurt from the inside out.

But I guessed I was going to live. Dammit.

"Hey, buddy, you all right?" A man wearing striped blue-gray coveralls was crouched down and looking at me under the boxcar. A railroad worker of some kind, all greasy looking.

"Never been better," I grumbled.

"You can't be under there. Ain't safe."

"Thanks for the tip." I touched my smarting mouth. I'd obviously been in a fight. My watch was gone. My wallet. Fuck! 10-31. I got robbed. Rolled like a damn bum. Yeah. Drinking was hard work.

Déjà vu on that thought. I'd said it out-loud not too long ago, to someone, before I blacked out.

The railroad man mumbled something, followed by the squelch of a receiver. His buddies would arrive soon, to drag the drunk out from under the boxcar.

I'd committed an arrestable offence, trespassing on railroad property. The fat lip told me I had help. Under any other circumstances, I might have laughed. I was already facing a murder rap. Anything less would be child's play.

Hardy har har.

The man knelt down again. "Come on out from under there, buster."

"Buster?" He must've been my ex-wife's brother. If I was up to the task, I'd have kicked his ass for calling me buster.

Tires crunched gravel. A car stopped. Through a swirl of dust, I saw the wheels. A Mercedes? I clumsily geckoed out from under the boxcar and discovered I was wrong. It was a Ford Crown Vic, white and blue, a Denver patrol car. Why had I'd envisioned a Mercedes?

My guts threatened to spill again.

Squinting, I looked around, saw nothing familiar about the layout. Last night, I must've staggered over here from the Star in a drunken stupor, got mugged and left for dead.

I tried to stand up, but dizziness tangled my feet, and I flopped back down in a huff.

"Stay there," the cop said.

I didn't recognize him, but I knew the drill. While he huddled with the railroad people, he pulled on surgical gloves, like I might give him the plague during the impending pat-down.

Made me feel microbial.

I sat up on the ground under a punishing sun and took stock of my once white shirt. The sleeves had been ripped, my belt pinched, pockets turned inside out, and what was left of my clothes stunk of booze, urine, and vomit. Proof positive I didn't drink for fun.

Another car pulled up, this time a black Crown Vic, kicking up dust. I coughed. Pain rifled through my ribcage. Now I knew how Adam felt when God ripped out a rib and made a woman. Probably a blonde, blue-eyed woman with sharp knees and C notes flying out of her bra.

I blinked. My brain must've been stewed last night, like grandma's tomatoes. Images swam in my gray matter that had no business being there.

The car door opened and out stepped the piss ant himself, Detective P-Peterson. Seeing me like this was going to make his day.

"What do you know? Jack Sabre in all his glory."

"Fuck you." There was no arguing my condition.

The patrol officer walked up. "Come on, buster." He yanked me to my feet and slammed me over the hood of his car. "You're going to jail."

Buster again. What was all this buster crap? My stomach made a threatening gurgle.

He cuffed my hands behind my back. "Got any ID?"

The hot hood was cooking my left earlobe. I looked at Peterson, standing by the fender with a fucking smirk on his face. "Tell him who I am."

"Never seen him before." His smirk morphed into a you-are-totally-fucked smile.

"Look at me. I got mugged, god dammit!"

The cop started pawing my pockets. "Got anything that's gonna stick me?" He searched my pant-legs, my soaked crotch. "You have the right to remain silent."

Still grinning, Peterson rocked back on his heels and clasped his hands behind his ass.

I didn't like the bastard yesterday, but my pounding brain couldn't recall why I hated him more today than ever.

"You have the right to an attorney."

My stomach lurched. I retched on the car hood.

"Hey!" the cop shouted and stepped back.

Lime green goo made a slow, sizzling crawl

across the hot hood. Even had chunks in it, probably from the knuckle sandwiches I'd eaten last night. I hacked up some more, spattering all over Peterson's cheap suit coat.

He screwed up his face and stumbled backward. His grin was gone.

Body fluids well spent.

I snorted, honked, and spit for added effect.

Chapter Six

THE JAIL DEPUTY GAVE me a mop and bucket, made me swab the floor of my own drunk-tank. I didn't know how long I'd been there, a year it seemed. My throat felt vomit raw, and every breath came with a shot of ribcage pain and a chaser of head banging. The sickening odor I smelled was coming from me.

Worse, I'd sobered up.

I dunked my mop in the bucket.

Like a faulty bulb in a cellar, haunting images flickered in my mind's eye: a beautiful woman, leather upholstery, a fast car, and a bad beating. Nothing connected. I blamed the knot on my head. A concussion, I guessed. Choppy recollections never accompanied any of my previous blackouts.

I slopped soapy water on the floor and

worked the mop back and forth. If only Maria could see me now. She'd understand how much losing her was killing me.

With any luck, last night would come back to me in all its nightmarish detail. Maybe I'd remember who took my watch and wallet.

I wasn't oblivious to the fact that my drinking had gotten out of control, but this was my first time in the slammer. Porky was right. I could end up like the bums in his bar. Who knows, Danny might become my best buddy.

But being drunk was good for me. I could withdraw into the past. Memories were my friends, Maria my companion once again in whiskey heaven.

Sober, I had no friends. Not like before, when I was a nice guy and everybody liked me. When I had Maria...when I had a life...before I became known as Black Jack. Now anger was my constant tormentor, gnawing at my insides like maggots on spoiled meat. Revenge. Justice. Hate.

Sober was lonely.

Sober was pain.

Sober was a hangover that would kill a moose.

"All right, buddy," the deputy said from behind the door. "We're gonna get you through booking."

I set aside the mop, nice and neat, the handle propped up against the wall.

Like last night.

When I was propped up against a fender.

A Mercedes.

Silver.

I shuddered. Where did that memory come from?

My head hurt.

"I need aspirin," I told the deputy.

The door clanked and swung open. "The nurse'll have a look at you." Stepping in, the deputy grimaced at the sight and smell of me. "But you gotta get cleaned up first."

He didn't touch me, just motioned to the door. A quick glance for anything left behind. I touched my back pocket. Empty. I remembered. The fuckers got my wallet. I had to call the bank, cancel my credit card.

"I need to use a phone."

"Later."

I had to get out of here. "When do I see the

judge?"

"You don't."

"How the fuck long do I have to stay—?"

"You're getting out, but if ya don't watch your mouth, I'll put you back in the tank."

"Okay, great, no problem." Never argue with good news.

I followed him down a polished hallway to a sign that read: *Booking*.

Prisoners shuffled by wearing orange jumpsuits. A couple deputies looked up from a clipboard, wrinkled their noses at me. I couldn't wait to get out of these stinking clothes.

The deputy stood me under bright lights. Streetlights? Why did I think of streetlights? Or was it a streetlight? It was a bright light. Maybe I had died and gone into the light.

The deputy handed me a placard with my name on it. "Face the camera."

I winced, ran a hand through my ratty hair, tried to suck in my fat lip. This wouldn't be a picture I'd send home to Mom.

The camera flashed. A bright light. Bright as a locomotive... Where did that recollection come from?

The fingerprint station next. No ink. A hand scan. My picture came up on the monitor. Positive ID. Jack Sabre. Denver PD. The technician looked at me like something he'd scrape off the bottom of his shoe.

Jesus. Everyone was a fuckin' critic. "I had a bad night."

"This way," the deputy said.

He walked me to an elevator. "You're goin' upstairs to shower."

"Suppose I have to wear an orange jumpsuit." I'd fit right in around here.

"Somebody brought you clean clothes."

"Somebody?" I didn't recall having a fairy godmother or guardian angel. "Who?"

"Some slick chick. Looks like she had money."

A hundred dollar bill flashed in my head. Long red fingernails. A leggy woman at the bar. Of course. I was in her car. The Mercedes. In the railroad yard.

"Was she a hooker?"

The guard huffed. "None of my business who posts bail."

"Business?"

I saw wild eyes behind a black ski mask. *Keep your nose out of our business.* That voice. I knew that voice. My knees buckled under me.

The deputy grabbed my arm, kept me upright. "Easy, Jack."

I was in more trouble than the last white man at the Alamo.

Chapter Seven

I STEPPED OUT OF CITY JAIL on the Cherokee Street side. My head still hurt, and my lip throbbed. My stomach felt like a chunk of granite. The clean clothes felt good, though, civilian clothes: jeans, cotton shirt, a bit on the baggy side, and Nikes that pinched my toes. If my rich benefactor was the hooker from last night, why had she set me up for a beating?

When I find her ass, that'll cost her plenty.

I hoofed it toward Colfax. The deputy had given me change for bus fare. There were still some good guys in the world.

I wasn't one of them.

In the shower, I'd remembered everything. Yeah. I was drunk. Peterson must've been counting on that, figured I wouldn't recognize him in a ski mask. He should've stuffed a dirty diaper in his mouth to disguise his voice.

I got the message. Stay out of their business. Whose business? What business? How was Maria involved?

And Vallinski, damn it, maybe I was right about him, after all. He could've killed Maria, and Peterson could have lied about the DNA not matching to throw off the investigation.

But why?

And what made him think that I'd keep my nose out of his business? The stupid son of a bitch didn't know me by now?

I made it to the corner on Fourteenth. A silver Mercedes pulled up to the curb.

My stomach turned from granite to gunpowder.

I stopped, stepped back. Heart hammering, I watched the tinted window roll down, expecting to see the barrel of a gun, a muzzle flash.

It was worse. I saw the blonde slut. She wore a beige blazer, white blouse, and men's trousers, looked more like a realtor than a hooker.

What was she, a goddamned chameleon?

She smiled. "Get in."

"Go fuck yourself." The last time I went

with that bitch I ended up the guest of honor at an ass-kicking party. I stormed off east on Fourteenth. She followed behind, driving slow.

"Don't be an ass, Jack," she shouted across the passenger seat. "I didn't know he was going to rough you up."

"Rough me up? You damn near got me killed."

"He told me he wanted to talk, that's all."

I remembered her tugging on Sasquatch's arm, telling him to stop. She obviously didn't have any clout with those guys. "Who was the muscle he brought with him?"

"Get in. I'll tell you."

I stopped.

She stopped.

Traffic honked and drove around her.

"I'm supposed to trust you now?"

"I got you out of jail, didn't I?"

"It's your fault that I got beat up and thrown in jail."

"Let me make it up to you."

"Great." I threw out my arms. "Give me back my Maria. All's forgiven."

She shook her head. "I can help you find

her killer."

"Vallinski killed her. Peterson lied about it."

"Who's Peterson?"

Yeah, right, who's Peterson? "How dumb do you think I am?" She had to know he was one of the goons at my beat-down. I couldn't be wrong about that. He's probably the one who sent her to fetch me from the Star, like the good little bitch she is, and led me straight to the dog at the other end of her leash. She knew more than she was letting on, but I couldn't trust anything she had to say.

Fool me once, shame on her; fool me twice, shame on me.

Besides, I didn't know her from Eve, but I had my ways of finding out whose garden she was playing in, sources that I trusted.

Still, I had to ask, "Who do you think killed Maria?"

"I don't know, but—"

"See, we've got nothing to talk about."

"Okay." She groaned. "I get it. You don't trust me."

"Sexy and smart, you should be named

Woman of the Year." I turned and started walking back toward Cherokee Street.

She threw the car into reverse and backed up after me. Tires screeched. Horns honked. I figured she must've had good insurance.

"Damn it. I'm trying to help you."

"What am I to you, some dumb cop you can lead around by the nose? I don't need your help."

Cars careened around her. "Stupid bitch!" some guy yelled.

She flipped him off. "Bet you didn't know the M-E found an envelope in Vallinski's pocket."

I stopped walking before she could wreck her Mercedes. "I don't care if he had the fuckin' Nobel Prize on him."

"Ten thousand dollars cash, old bills, tens and twenties."

That got my attention. "A payoff?"

"See? You're not such a dumb cop, after all."

"How is it you're privy to that kind of information?"

"I have friends in low places."

I knew it. She'd rather jack me around than

give me a straight answer. Nothing but a waste of my time.

"Will you get in now?"

"I'd sooner hump a rattlesnake."

"Why do you have to be so mean, Jack?"

"I don't like you. That reason enough?"

She actually looked hurt. "Fine."

The Mercedes tore off. I made note of the plate.

RKMYWRLD.

"A payoff?" I mumbled. Proof there were more bastards involved in Maria's murder than just Vallinski. But who? And what were they up to that got Maria killed?

Terry Wright

Chapter Eight

I GOT BACK TO MY APARTMENT just before noon and headed straight for the medicine cabinet. After a handful of aspirin and a shot of bourbon, I'd be ready to rock and roll in no time.

Next to my bed I kept a loaded Colt .38 snubbie. An ankle-holster in the nightstand drawer. Lots of extra bullets. Armed again, I pulled my pant leg down over the gun and felt like Linus with his security blanket, nice and cozy.

Now for my cell phone. It wasn't fancy. Nothing smart about it. When I bought it, I thought the camera feature might come in handy. It didn't. I plucked the phone from its charger dock on the kitchen counter. Flipped it open. Pushed a speed dial button.

Chad Brendon's number. The good old boy was still a beat cop. Sometimes I wished I still was

~66~

too.

"Jack, you all right?"

No fooling caller ID. "I need a favor."

"You need a lawyer."

"Besides that. Run a plate for me."

"Ah...Jack. It's against regulations—"

"Fuck regulations. Some hot blonde bailed me out of jail. I need to know who she is."

"Why?"

"She's got inside information on Maria's murder investigation."

"Let me get a pen."

I leaned against the counter, wondering how long it would take Chad to get me a name.

"What's the plate number?"

"R-K-M-Y-W-R-L-D."

Silence.

"Chad?"

"You sure? Rock my world?"

"No, I'm guessing. What the hell do you think?"

"It can't be."

"It was on a silver Mercedes."

Chad exhaled so hard I thought he'd been knifed in the back.

"Talk to me, buddy."

"I've got bad news for you, Jack. That's Helen Hodges' car."

My throat tightened. "As in Mayor Hodges?"

"His daughter."

"Son of a bitch!"

"What?"

"I thought she was just a fuckin' high priced hooker."

"What does she know about Maria's murder?"

"I don't know, but I'm sure of one thing. This case stinks all the way up to City Hall."

"Don't do anything stupid, Jack."

I flipped the phone shut. Nothing like a shot of adrenaline to kill what was left of my hangover.

My fat lip still throbbed, a grim reminder of why I should stop drinking.

Clue number one. Ten thousand dollars. Small bills. In an envelope on Vallinski's body. When I'd visited his mother, she'd said someone owed him money. He'd gone to the donut shop on Kalamath to collect. It didn't take a brain surgeon to know where to start this investigation.

Pilots have a rule: eight hours from bottle to throttle. Bikers don't. I shrugged into my leather jacket and grabbed the Harley keys off the kitchen table. Riding gloves came out of the front pocket, cell phone went in.

Easy Rider, eat your heart out.

I stepped from the apartment's express elevator and headed across the underground garage. Gloves on, I straddled my Harley Sportster. The gas tank was painted glitter-hot red, pinstriped in black, and chrome alloy wheels made her sparkle on the highway. With one push of a button, I got her started, ramming thunder in my ears and an earthquake between my legs.

Sunglasses on, I blasted out of the garage and roared down Colfax, headed east toward Kalamath. Colorado, in all its infinite legislative wisdom, didn't require motorcycle riders to wear helmets. I took full advantage of that, in spite of the fact that riders without helmets often ended up organ donors.

Since Maria died, I didn't give a damn.

The donut shop sat at the east end of a dogleg strip mall. I pulled the Sportster into a parking slot in front of the Mexican restaurant next door and dropped the kickstand. As I dismounted, I removed my sunglasses, just like Arnold Schwarzenegger in *The Terminator*.

Entering the donut shop, I held the door for an exiting patron, white bag of donuts clutched to her chest like precious jewels. Stepping inside, I got in the *Order Here* line and inhaled sugary air. Nothing smelled as sweet as a donut shop. Especially on an empty stomach.

The offerings were colorful and plenty, enormous donuts displayed in neat rows on trays set inside a curved glass display counter, a mouthwatering shrine to sugar and calories. A saloon-like gate allowed passage from the front area to the narrow space behind the counter. Along the back wall, more glass displays, brightly lit and inviting, showed off huge apple fritters and cinnamon rolls on trays angled just right for perfect viewing.

A bone-white door to the backroom swung open, and a big-mustached Mexican stepped out carrying a full tray of donuts. The white apron he wore seemed in stark contrast to his bulk; he could've been a bouncer instead of a baker. After swapping trays in the display case, he retreated to the back. I peered through the small window in the door, hoping to get a glimpse of the kitchen but didn't see much, a square metal vat, the donut cooker probably, a long table dusted with flour.

When it was my turn to order, a teenager behind the counter said, "May I help you, sir?" She wore her hair in a net, and her ears were pierced from top to bottom and adorned with silver rings. Her white gown smelled sugary sweet.

I glanced around like any prospective donut eater but fought the urge to purchase something. "I want to see your boss."

"She comes in at four in the morning."

My stomach growled. I scanned the glass encased shelves of Bear Claws and Long Johns. "Who's in charge when she's not here?"

"Me."

It took a moment to process that information. The kid didn't look like she could be in charge of a doll house kitchen. But then again, how hard was selling donuts? I cocked my head toward the display on my left. "Are those Long Johns cream filled?"

"Custard."

"You know a guy named Martin Vallinski?"

"Never heard of him."

"Scruffy looking guy, wiry hair. Bad clothes. He was here the other day. Picked up an envelope."

"Maybe you'd like a jelly filled Bizmark? We have them glazed and sprinkled with powdered sugar."

Tempting. "Anybody pick up an envelope or drop one off?"

"I just sell donuts, mister."

"Yeah." I smacked my lips and eyed the Bizmarks. Just one would give me a sugar rush. Two would send me to the moon. I pulled off my gloves to get cash from my pocket. "What's your boss's name?"

"Her business cards are right there." She pointed to a card holder on the counter, tucked up next to the register.

I took a card. "Bag me up a couple of those glazed Bizmarks." I peeled a ten spot off my wad of ones.

She smiled.

My stomach would've high-fived me if it could have.

While she bagged the goods, I glanced at the card:

Lila Peterson. Owner.

Peterson? My guts pretzeled. As in Detective Benny Peterson? Was Lila his wife? His sister? His mother? Was this just a coincidence or was he somehow involved with Martin Vallinski? After all, someone here knew him. Why else would Benny Peterson drag his feet in the investigation of Maria's murder: to protect Lila? Maybe he was a dirty cop. Maria must've found out...got herself killed —

"Here you go." The teenager handed me a little white bag. "That'll be four-eighty."

"For two donuts?"

"We use real sugar."

I glanced to the backroom door. The Mexican's face filled the small window, scowling, like maybe he would bounce me out on my ass if I complained too loudly.

Handing her the ten spot, I got a different whiff of this donut shop. Something stunk to high heaven.

Chapter Nine

THE EXHAUST PIPES angling off my V-Twin engine were illegal in Denver, made enough noise to sling a decibel meter needle to Wyoming, so I coasted the Sportster into the parking lot at Precinct Four. No sense making a noisy entrance, no matter how pissed off I was. Captain Salvador would have me arrested if I so much as squeaked too loud, but I had to clue him in about Peterson.

Folding my sunglasses into my coat pocket, I took a quick breath. My stomach felt like it was trying to digest a hot brick. I pocketed my gloves and bounded through the front doors as if I still belonged there. Once a cop. Always a cop. Take my badge. Take my gun. I still had chasing bad guys in my blood.

Sitting at her desk, Miss Mina Finetree looked up at me over the black rim of her glasses.

The disdain on her face couldn't have been worse if she'd found dog shit on her patio. "What are you doing here, Jack?"

"I have to see the captain."

"You have a death wish?"

"Just tell him I'm here."

"He's busy—"

"Fuck that." I stormed to his office...

"Don't go in there—"

...and pushed through the door. Bad move. I'd startled him off some woman lying on his desk, white skirt hiked up around her belly button and her knees splayed in the air.

"Jack! What the hell?" He angled his butt to me as he struggled to get his underwear up from around his ankles.

The bimbo let out a mousey squeal. Her knees snapped together like Tyrannosaurus jaws, but I wasn't scoping out her bush. My eyes were locked on her erect nipples, swollen as little red rose buds. My first thought was to turn away, but seeing the captain in a compromising position was reason enough to root me to the carpet. "Well, well, well—"

"Shut up, Jack." Salvador zipped his

zipper.

The babe got her boobs stuffed back into her bra. "Ever hear of knocking?"

Fuck her...oh-oh...too late. "Hanky-panky on duty, Captain? What's up with that?"

"It's not what it looks like."

"Of course it's what it looks like." I advanced toward the desk, hoping to boost the embarrassment factor off the Richter scale. "Afternoon delight is afternoon delight."

The babe hopped down from the desk and smoothed her skirt, seemingly content to go commando.

Salvador got his belt buckled. "What do you want?"

"Internal Affairs wouldn't be happy to hear—"

"I don't have to explain anything to them...or you." He guided the babe toward the door in such a rush her sweater got left behind. After a peck on the cheek, she slipped out the door quicker than Monica Lewinski slipped out of her dress.

Salvador escaped to his cushy high-backed chair. "You're not supposed to be here, Jack."

I leaned against his desk where the babe's white sweater was spread out to pad her backside. "And you're not supposed to be fuckin' the hired help."

"Look—"

"No, you look. I only came here to tell you Peterson is dirty."

"Get out."

"I don't know how deep in the shit he's standing, but you'd better have an independent investigator recheck Maria's case file. You'll find some things that don't jive."

"Jive?"

"The DNA under Maria's fingernails that didn't match Vallinski's, for starters. Did you see the test results yourself?"

"I read the forensic report."

"It's been doctored."

"The crime lab wouldn't do that."

"Somebody did. And Vallinski had ten grand on him."

"How did you find out about that?"

"A little birdie told me." *The mayor's daughter, tweet, tweet.* "Vallinski picked up that money from the donut shop, which, by the way, is owned by a woman named Lila Peterson. Could that name be a coincidence? I doubt it. I think she's related to Detective Peterson."

"She's his sister."

"You know her?"

"Peterson had mentioned her."

"He paid Vallinski to kill Maria, and he's derailed the investigation at every turn. Falsified evidence—"

"You'd better have some solid proof before you go blabbing that around."

I didn't have squat for proof, just a gut-crushing hunch. "I'll get the proof." I leaned over his desk, over the abandoned sweater, the scene of carnal knowledge interrupted. "Don't you worry about that—"

A familiar and unexpected aroma stopped me. Sugary sweet...coming from...? I grabbed the sweater off the desktop, looked at Salvador then pressed the knitted material to my face.

And inhaled.

Nothing smelled as sweet...as a donut shop. "Son of a whore!"

Panic creased Salvador's brow. "Now don't go off half cocked, Jack."

I pointed to the door, pissed that my finger was shaking. "That was Lila Peterson." I stormed around the desk. "Tell me you didn't know her, you lying prick." I yanked Salvador out of the chair by his shirt collars. "What are you doin' fucking Peterson's sister?"

"At my age, I take it when I can get it."

"You should have locked the door."

"I didn't say I was any good at it."

I wanted to knock him into next Tuesday. "She's involved in Maria's killing. How could you...?" The next thought hit my brain like a sledgehammer. "You...you're involved." I shook him. "Maria was your daughter, for Christsake."

"You've got it all wrong, Jack."

I yanked him nose-to-nose. "Then set me straight, right now."

"It's not your case."

The adrenaline blast in my bloodstream made me dizzy with rage. "I'm makin' it my case."

"You've been warned, Jack. Stay out of it."

"Warned?" I'd have shot him if my fists weren't full of cop collars and my gun wasn't holstered so far down my leg. "You know about the rail-yard beating I got?"

"Maria's dead. Nothing we do can bring her back."

"So I'm supposed to stick my head in the toilet and let Peterson shit all over the justice system. He's not getting away with it." I shoved Salvador back into the chair. It rolled into the wall, knocking pictures and trophies to the floor. "He's going down. And if I find out you're part of the problem, you're going down with him."

"This case is bigger than you think, Jack."

"Maria's gone forever, damn it. Nothing's bigger than that."

"I don't want you getting killed, too."

"Remember the Alamo, motherfucker."

He frowned. "What's that supposed to mean?"

"The last man fought to the death."

"Don't do it, Jack!"

I slammed the door on my way out.

"When are you ever gonna listen to me?" he shouted through the closed door.

Mina Finetree sat behind her desk, polishing her fingernails. "I told you not to go in there." She smiled like a schoolmarm.

I needed a drink.

Chapter Ten

TIMES LIKE THESE MADE whiskey's pull irresistible, as if getting bombed would somehow make my torment go away. Make Maria come back. Make sense of Salvador and Lila Peterson, the fuck buddies of Precinct Four. Make Benny Peterson a clean cop. Make Martin Vallinski deserving of the grave I'd put him in.

However, there was no making sense of Helen Hodges. The mayor's daughter, for Christsake. She'd gotten me beat up, thrown in jail, and then out of the blue, she'd bailed me out and expected me to trust her. My gut told me she was one of the bad guys. For all I knew, I was next on their to-do-away-with list.

Gunning my Sportster engine produced a deafening roar that echoed down the alley of old red brick, barred windows, and warehouse garage doors. I blasted up to the Star Bar's back door and dropped the kick stand, just ten feet from the chain-link fence and wooden trash enclosure where Porky's patrons went to pee.

Pushing my way inside, the familiar rank and gloomy watering hole embraced me like a ghostly lover.

I was back on hallowed ground.

Porky stood fat-bellied behind the bar, thumbing through a swimsuit issue of Sports Illustrated. He glanced up. His face drooped. "I don't want no trouble, Jack."

The place was vacant as a corpse's stare. No drunks to head-bash with a bottle, no babe to take me to an ass whooping.

I took off my gloves and slapped them on the bar. "Hit me with a double."

Porky slammed a coffee mug in front of me and turned to the pot on the hotplate. "You're still cut off."

I peeled off my sunglasses. "Don't bullshit with me. I'm not in the mood."

"Try this." He poured coffee in the mug. "You've gotta stay sober, Jack. Stay focused."

Odd statement from a man whose

livelihood was serving booze. "I want to get drunk, stay UN-focused, that's the whole point of drinking."

"And feel sorry for yourself again. I hate to tell you this, Jack, but you're not the only swinging dick to lose someone he loved."

"Swinging dick?"

"Life is about losing." He replaced the coffee pot on the hotplate. "Everybody dies, Jack. Trick is to not do the dying yourself."

Porky was living proof that a good bartender had to be a good shrink, as well. My sixth cop-sense kicked in. He was trying to tell me something without really telling me. "You know something I don't know?"

"I've heard things."

"What things?"

"You don't know who you can trust anymore." He leaned his fat forearms on the bar. "Like Captain Salvador."

"What do you know about Salvador?"

Porky grinned. "Let's just say he likes donuts more than your ordinary cop."

"Donuts?" I played dumb to see how much he'd tell me.

"He's doing Lila Peterson."

Seemed I must've been the last to know. I grabbed the coffee mug and wished it was straight Kentucky bourbon. "How do you know about Lila Peterson?"

A woman's voice answered from behind me. "I told him, Jack."

I spun on my barstool. Helen Hodges. This time she was dressed all business-like, tan blazer, tan slacks, white blouse buttoned up proper. The glare from the window behind her haloed her body in angelic light. I had a million questions to ask her, but I wasn't about to play into her charms. She got me beat up, god dammit. Being nice to her wasn't an option. "Not you again."

She strode to my side and placed a dainty hand on my leather-jacketed shoulder. There couldn't have been a more conflicted connection between two people. "Are you still mad at me, Jack?"

"I'd rather chum up to a gator." I swigged the coffee like it was a shot of Old Crow and scalded the roof of my mouth. Gritting my teeth, I swallowed fire. Every time this woman came near me I ended up in pain.

She sat on the barstool to my left. "Maria was my friend."

I exhaled heat. It wasn't hard to believe my wife would befriend the mayor's daughter-slash-hooker-wannabe, but to not mention her, not once ever, seemed a stretch for the likes of friendship. An acquaintance maybe, that's all. "How did you two know each other?"

"I'm Helen Hodges, but you already know that, don't you."

"Answer the question."

"We volunteered at the mission together."

She was referring to the Denver Rescue Mission on Park Avenue. Maria had helped out there, with meals for the homeless. Mother Theresa's heart wasn't any bigger than my Maria's. "So why's the mayor's daughter fraternizing with the likes of Martin Vallinski?"

"My father insisted I help the less fortunate. Builds character, he'd said. Maria did it out of kindness in her heart."

"If she hadn't worked at the mission, she wouldn't have met Vallinski, and she'd still be alive today."

"Martin earned his meals sometimes, doing

odd jobs around the place."

"What did he do to earn ten grand?" I sipped my coffee, slowly this time, real cool like, expecting her to confirm a payoff for killing Maria. Porky would be my witness.

"It's not what you think, Jack."

Another runaround. "It is what I think. He killed Maria, and Peterson paid him ten grand to do it."

"Who's Peterson?"

"Don't play the dumb blonde role with me." I wished Porky would eighty-six her for thinking I was stupid, but he just stood there polishing shot glasses...he never polished the glasses. "Detective Benny Peterson. Don't deny you know him."

"Lila's father. Sure. But I've never met him."

I was amazed at how she could lie without even blinking. "He's investigating Maria's murder. He wants me to stay out of it, told me so in the rail yard the other night." I pointed to my busted lip. "Remember now?"

"It wasn't him."

"I recognized his voice."

"You were drunk, Jack."

"I know what I heard. I just don't know why you're protecting him."

"Think, Jack. How could you have solved Maria's murder so quickly when Peterson hasn't been able to crack the case for six months?"

"Because he's been dragging his ass and doctoring evidence, that's how come."

"It's not that simple."

I squeezed the coffee mug to keep from throwing it across the bar. Keeping a conversation with her on track was like steering a Mack truck through a mud bog. "What was the ten grand for, a payoff to kill Maria, right?"

"A payoff, yes." She swallowed. "But not for Maria's murder. It was a down payment...on another murder."

Porky stopped polishing.

I stopped breathing. Had Maria gotten wind of an assassination plot? Maybe the conspirators killed her to keep her quiet. Was she living a Stephen Coonts novel but didn't make it to chapter five? Why hadn't she come to me in chapter four?

Helen tisk-tisk-tisked me. "You screwed

that up by killing Vallinski, the hired gun."

Setting down the coffee mug, I stared into the black dregs. Maria was dead. Vallinski was dead. And someone was alive who would have been dead if I hadn't shot the bastard. "Who was he supposed to kill?"

"Come on, Jack." Helen leaned forward. "If I knew that I'd be talking to the FBI right now...not some washed up cop with his life in a bottle."

I'd had enough of her insults and turned to face her. "You say you know shit, and then you don't know shit. I'm—"

I caught a whiff of her perfume, subtle yet magnetic.

"I'm..."

And up close like this, her beautiful blue eyes drew me in like a crow to road-kill. I couldn't breathe.

"I'm..."

I fought the sudden urge to gather her in my arms and kiss her...same as when I'd met Maria, that instinctive tug of desire. My God, what was I thinking? How could I even think it?

Stop, Jack, before you do something stupid.

I tore my gaze from her face. The pounding

in my chest felt as alarming as a heart attack. My hand went to Maria's carved name on the bar-top. I stroked the grooved M, the upside-down hearts and arrows of the A's, the R and the I. It suddenly seemed written in a foreign language.

I'm sorry, Maria. I'm sorry—

"Jack?"

I gritted my teeth and dragged my brain out of the pity gutter. "You better come straight with me, Helen, here and now. About everything—"

"So you will? You'll help me figure this out?"

"Everything, Helen, or I'll see you go down with Peterson and the whole bunch."

"Anything you want to know."

That remained to be seen, so I put her to the test. "How is it that you know so much about this case? You got someone on the inside?"

"I do."

"Who?"

Another female voice popped into the room. "Me."

Oh Jesus. I'd know that voice anywhere. I didn't turn around to face her, just looked up at

Porky. "You've got to be shittin' me."

He shrugged. "You don't have to do this alone, Jack."

"This ain't Charlie's Angels, for cryin' out loud."

"More like Mission Impossible," Mina Finetree said and claimed the barstool on my right. Seemed Salvador's receptionist had been doing some counterintelligence of her own.

"Why are you spying on your boss?"

"Maria was my friend, too." She nodded hello to Helen, as if we'd all just sat down for a friendly game of Bridge. "How do you like your new partners?"

"Partners?"

"Angels," Porky put in.

"Charlie had three. I saw the show." I glanced at Helen on my left, sharp, professional, sexy, and then back at Mina, the epitome of librarian smart-hood and cool as a summer salad. A guy could do worse for partners...er...angels. "We're short one."

"Take what you can get, Jack," Porky said in his usual counselor-firm voice.

I slid the coffee mug toward him. "Better

freshen this up, my man. We're going to be here a while."

***

We moved to the front-most table, about as far from the broken john as we could get without talking in the street. Porky poured a round of coffee for the three of us. Funny how I didn't thirst for the hard stuff like I usually did this time of the afternoon. I had to keep my head screwed on straight, though all the caffeine in my bloodstream had given me a severe case of the jitters.

"So you're the leak," I said to Mina.

"Captain Salvador doesn't know that I'm on to him."

"On to him? Salvador? I'm more interested in Peterson. He's the turd in this toilet."

Helen set her mug on the marred tabletop. "They know more about Maria's murder than they're letting on."

"Off the record stuff," Mina added.

I shot her a bulls-eye glare. "As in...?"

"They know who had her killed. I'm sure of it. Peterson says he's working on an arrest affidavit."

"But you haven't seen it, right?"

"No."

"So I'm right. Peterson is stonewalling the investigation. But why?"

Helen jumped in. "It's an election year."

Politicians and I didn't mix. They were just a bunch of liars looking for dishonest work. Crooks, yes...but murderers, probably not. Union bosses, maybe. Ask Jimmy Hoffa. But Maria, sweet Maria would have no more use for them than a busted windshield. "Why do you think there's a connection to politics?"

"Because your little stunt the other day attracted some high powered attention."

"Over that lowlife son of a bitch? Why would anybody give a snot rag about what happened to Vallinski?"

Helen shrugged. "Somebody got pissed off enough to beat the crap out of you."

"It was Peterson."

Helen glanced at Mina.

"It's okay." Mina touched Helen's blazer sleeve. "Tell him."

Her face sagged like she was about to confess to murder. "His name is Johnny Harman, the guy you met in the railroad yard the other night."

"He sounded like Peterson."

"You were drunk."

"Don't remind me."

"Harman was supposed to talk to you about Maria's case. Instead, he brought some muscle with him. I had no idea."

I was still stuck on Johnny Harman. "Who the fuck is he?"

Mina glowered over the top of her Clark Kent glasses. "You've got to get out more, Jack."

"The movies, the gay bars, out where?"

"He's the election campaign manager for Ray Davis," Helen said.

"Davis." That name set off alarm bells. "The audio-visual tycoon...he went bankrupt when the city changed over to digital technology."

"And now the bastard is after my dad's job."

Mina chimed in. "If he's mayor, he'll bankrupt the city to even the score."

I shrugged. "He can't win an election in this town."

"He's running second in the polls."

I gripped my coffee mug... "Second only means he's the first loser." ...lifted it to my lips.

Helen grabbed my arm, stopped me from drinking. "He's going to start a smear campaign, make my dad look really bad."

"So? Dirty politics as usual. Bash your opponent. Make yourself look better. Most people recognize that crap and ignore the lies."

"My dad hasn't done anything wrong, anything bad for the city. He's been a good mayor."

"So what could Davis have on your dad? Something from his past?"

She let go of my arm. "Anything would be a lie."

"Helen," Mina jumped in. "Your dad's reelection isn't the point here."

"It's a motive for murder."

My coffee-toasted brain couldn't wrap itself around the connection. "Why would Davis have to kill Maria to win the election? That's crazy?"

"Maybe Maria had something on Davis," Mina said.

My vision started skipping frames. Damn caffeine. I'd need a whole bottle of Old Crow to calm my nerves. "So you're suggesting Davis sent Harman to scare me off the case because the more I dug into Maria's past, the more likely I'd find some dirt on him."

"It's a place to start," Mina said.

Good as any. "Then we need to know who paid Vallinski ten grand."

Helen glanced into her coffee mug. "That could give us a lead on who he was supposed to kill."

"Your dad, maybe?" I'd said it out loud without thinking.

Helen's face blanched. "Jack, don't say that."

"I wouldn't put it past Davis," Mina said. "The guy is a prick."

That word coming from Mina about knocked me out. I didn't know she had it in her...kind of a turn on... "We need to find a connection to Vallinski."

"Who would know him best?" Mina asked. "His past, his friends, his hangouts?"

"His mother," Helen said. "That's who." She looked at me with those icy blues. "You've got to talk to her, Jack."

My heart jumped into my throat and hung there like a worthless piece of meat.

He killed my boy. The old woman's words haunted me.

The last person in the world I wanted to face was Mrs. Vallinski, but to get to the truth, I'd have to suffer her wrath up close and personal.

Chapter Eleven

THE SKY WAS GETTING DARK. I chugged my Harley up to the curb in front of Mrs. Vallinski's house on Galapago just north of Eight Avenue. A dim light glowed behind the curtains.

Engine off. Kickstand down.

My heart pumped liquid dread. I'd rather be in a shootout with heavily armed bank robbers than stalking up the sidewalk to this old lady's porch. I was here before, the day I killed her son. Now I was back to ask for her help.

The drone of traffic on nearby Santa Fe Drive irritated the evening air. I caught a whiff of barbeque smoke coming from next door. Children squealed in a backyard across the street. The city seemed different this time of night, sober as I was.

I stepped to the front door, porch boards creaking under my biker boots. A jagged-edged rip in the screen stared at me like the snarl of a guard dog.

He killed my boy.

I'll never forget her face when she'd screamed those words at me, the gritty strain of anger on her lips, the hard lines of grief on her brow, her swollen eyes red from a sleepless night of sorrow. I should shoot Martin Vallinski again for what he'd made me do to his mother.

I balled a fist and knocked hard. Footsteps approached. The doorknob squeaked. I braced myself for the coming storm. This would be a lot easier if I were drunk enough to not give a shit.

The door opened with a woody grunt, spearing a crack of light across my face. A frizzy-haired silhouette froze in the maw of the backlit gap. Her breathing sounded canine. "What're you doin' here?"

I had to force words from my gravel-lined throat. "Mrs. Vallinsky, I'm really sorry—"

"Ain't you caused me enough trouble already?" she growled out, her voice husky for such a petite frame.

"I need to talk to you about Martin."

"He was my only boy," she shouted.

The porch light blazed on, made me squint. Worse, it illuminated the old woman's face, her sunken eyes and houndish jowls. It could been years of hard living that gouged out all her wrinkles. Could have been an out of control son... "He fell into some bad company, ma'am. I'm hoping you'll help me find out who they are. Bring them to justice."

"And whose gonna bring you to justice, Jack?"

Perry Mason couldn't have stated her case any better...or louder.

I looked up at the weather-rotted porch ceiling for guidance from above, got nothing, then glanced down to my boots. "The devil, I assume, but until then, I've got a job to do."

"You ain't working for the cops no more. What are you talkin' about, job to do?"

I thought the whole neighborhood could hear her now. "Will you help me anyway?"

"Why should I?" She bellowed. "You killed my boy."

"Hey!" The next door neighbor waddled up to the porch rail. He wore a barbeque apron, clutched a spatula in one hand and a beer bottle in the other. The Mexican could've been Porky's brother. "This guy bothering you, Mrs. V?"

"Police business," I told him. "Buzz off."

"He ain't no cop," she said, all down her nose at me. "He's a trespasser."

"You don't look like a cop," the nosey neighbor noted.

"Undercover," I told him.

"He killed Martin," she tossed out.

"I'll call 911 for you, Mrs. V."

"I'm not leaving until I get some answers."

"We'll see about that." He stormed toward his house.

Think fast, Jack... I yanked open the screen door and towered over the old woman. "Martin had ten grand on him, money he was paid to kill someone."

Her eyes flashed with fear.

"I need to find out who paid him before they hire another gun. If I don't, someone is going to die."

She stood frozen in place and looked up at me like grandma looking up at the big bad wolf.

"I can't stop the murder if I'm in jail. Help me out here a little, please."

She blinked like the attic lights were flickering in her brain. "My boy wouldn't kill anyone."

"He killed my wife." Okay, maybe that was iffy at this point, but I said it with conviction.

She leaned out the door and craned her neck toward the neighbor's house. "It's okay, Eduardo. Nevermind callin' the cops."

He'd already made it to his front door. "You sure, Mrs. V?"

"Go back to your cookin'." She looked up at me with drafty eyes. "You comin' in or ain't you?"

How Martin ever took a wrong turn with this tough-talking woman for a mother I'd never know.

She backed off, gave me room to step inside.

My boots landed on a patterned throw rug. Soft lighting reflected off the polished hardwood floor with a museum-quality shine. The overheated air smelled of talcum powder and burnt toast. I unzipped my leather jacket and scanned the room. Crosses adorned the walls, an elaborate collection, and pictures of Jesus among photos of Martin: a baby, a boy, a young man wearing his army uniform, but nothing recent, nothing to reflect how his life had turned out, only how she wanted to remember him.

She closed the door behind me. "Can I get you somethin' to drink? Big K soda? Can't afford Coca-Cola, you know. Thank God for Walmart. Got some orange juice left over from supper."

"You had orange juice for supper?" The cop in me kept noticing things. No TV in the room. Not a speck of dust anywhere.

"Never heard of having breakfast for supper?" She moved toward the kitchen all shiny clean beyond the doorway. "Eggs and toast? Pancakes?"

No books. No magazines.

"I'm more of a meat and potato man."

"Wait 'til you get old and can't afford all that fancy food. You thirsty or ain't you?"

"No, I'm good, thanks." I still had a caffeine ringer going off in my head. And all this yakking about nothing wasn't going to get me out of here any sooner. "Did you know who Martin hung out with?"

"Riffraff, the whole bunch of them." She settled into a padded chair.

Tissue box on the armrest, nearly empty, and for good reason. A closed laptop sat on the table next to her. Power cord. Wireless mouse. Seemed a bit techie for this simple decor.

"Anybody seem out of place, anyone wearing suits or driving fancy cars? Anyone pick him up? Drop him off?"

"Not that I seen." She cocked her head toward the couch. "You gonna sit down or what?"

I stepped up to the laptop. Could be a wealth of information in there. "Is this his?"

"It's mine. I go online a lot. What of it?"

For an old woman, she seemed well connected. My mom couldn't spell computer much less use one. "Email?"

"Mostly how we kept in touch." She folded her veiny hands in her lap. "He was a good kid in that way, always lookin' out for his momma. That's why I can't see him killin' anybody."

The more I learned about Martin Vallinski, the more I began to think the same thing. I had to get my hands on those DNA tests. Note to self. *Mina Finetree, get the original DNA report from the lab.*

Mrs. Vallinski sniffled. She blew her nose in

a tissue.

Maybe I should've listened to Maria when she touched my shoulder just before I shot him. She wasn't a coconspirator; she was trying to stop me. I sat on the edge of the couch, bent forward, elbows on my knees, looking straight at Mrs. Vallinski. "All the evidence pointed to your son as my wife's killer. But the lead detective on the case wouldn't get an arrest warrant. The DA wouldn't commit to a trial."

"So you took justice with your own gun."

Though the truth of the matter was ugly, a lie here would be uglier. "I did. I set out to kill him, revenge, you know, but when I had him in my gun sights, I changed my mind. I couldn't kill him, not in cold blood. That's when he pulled a gun of his own. He gave no choice."

"You were chasing him," she spat. "He was scared."

I pointed to the photographs of Martin around us. "That boy was scared, Mrs. Vallinski, but the man he turned out to be wasn't afraid of breaking the law. He wasn't afraid to take a human life. That's what got him killed. Not me."

"I suppose you're right." She dabbed her

eyes with the tissue. "That boy made his own bed, even if he pissed in it."

"Then help me find out who paid him ten grand."

She honked into the tissue. "He mentioned his boss a few times, got paid in cash. Slipped me a C note every so often."

Dirty money, selling drugs probably, but I wouldn't tell her that. I'd tainted the image of her son enough.

"Who's going to take care of me now?" She sobbed.

I exhaled a long breath. Even scumbags were needed by someone. "Did he ever mention his boss by name?"

"Yeah." She sniffed. "Boss."

"A street name?"

"How should I know?"

Note to self: *Helen Hodges. Find out who on the street goes by that name.*

"I'd like to see Martin's room, if that's okay."

"His room?" She blew her nose. "It's my sewin' room now. Pick up a little extra money under the table. You won't turn me in to the IRS, would you?"

"No." The way this woman babbled on, seemed she wasn't running with all her wheels on both tracks.

"He hasn't had a room here for years."

But he must've been here earlier that day I came over. How else would she have known he went to the donut shop? "What was he doing here the day he died?"

"His laundry. It's still in there." She cocked her head toward the back of the house. "He got a call on his cell phone and left in a hurry. I just can't bear to touch his clothes." More tears. "Not yet. Not for a while."

"May I have a look?"

"Down the hall off the kitchen. On your right. I keep the door closed. You'll know why when you get there."

I got up and moved through the house toward the back room, taking notes as I went. Calendar on the kitchen wall. *Good Housekeeping.* Three days were marked off with black Xs since the day I shot her son. Empty coffee pot on the counter, clean as if never used. Flower-print wallpaper all down the hall. More crosses.

Bathroom door open. Shower curtain closed. Towels hotel neat.

I opened the laundry room door.

The stink hit me right between the eyes, sweaty socks and shitty drawers. Sewer soiled clothes were scattered helter-skelter across the floor. No wonder Mrs. Vallinski couldn't touch them. I wouldn't if I were her. Storage shelves were stacked floor to ceiling. Boxes. Stuffed plastic bags. T-shirts cluttered a counter for folding clothes. Ironing board against the wall. Drier door open, empty. Washer lid up, wet laundry inside.

I'd stepped into an alien world compared to the rest of the house. None of his mom's neat-freakishness had worn off on him. He'd definitely been in the middle of a major project when he took off to meet his death.

I'd heard it said that moving a single grain of sand on the beach could change the history of the world. If he hadn't gone to the donut shop, this room would probably be as tidy as the rest of the house. Instead, it was a legacy to his passing. A monument of sorts. If I were Mrs. Vallinski, I'd keep this door closed, as well.

Since Karen and I divorced, I'd done my

own laundry, even when Maria was alive. I'd told her she wasn't my maid. One chore I always did before tossing my pants into the washer was rummage through my pockets to make sure they were empty. Betting the procedure was universal, I inspected the room for any such pile of pocket dregs.

On the third shelf up, I found what I was looking for, a handful of odd scraps of paper and cash register receipts; I'd go through them later: a business card, Lila Peterson, who else? Gum wrappers, a matchbook from the Big Bunny Motel, the number one suicide palace in Lakewood, and the ever-present nests of pocket lint. At the risk of suffering a mortal illness, I deposited the items into my jacket pocket and returned to the front room where the breathing was easier.

"Find anything?" She had the laptop open on her lap, which made me think:

"Where does he keep his computer, you know, to email you?"

"Library. They have lots of them."

No help there. "Cell phone?"

"He took it with him, one of them pay in advance phones."

That struck me as odd. Helen made no mention of a cell phone among his personal effects. Just the envelope. And the gun. The phone must've slipped her mind. Or it wasn't on him. He could have left it here, which meant it would be in the laundry room. I'd have to go back in there and actually rummage through his filthy clothes. Touch them. Put my hands in the pockets. The thought made my stomach backfire. "You sure he had it with him?"

"Like I said, he took a call on it just before he left. I saw him put it in his pocket."

I hashed that around in my brain. If she was right, it meant that someone had pocketed the cell phone. Helen Hodges knew about the envelope with the ten grand. Mina Finetree was her inside contact. She'd told Helen about the money, so Mina had to know about the phone. Maybe she'd taken it...or knew of someone else who had it. Or maybe someone got to it first. The phone number of the person who'd informed Martin of the drop at the donut shop would be stored in the phone. That would be indisputable evidence fingering the person I was looking for, the person who'd made the down payment on the hit. A person who had access to dead people's stuff.

A cop.

Peterson or Salvador? One of them paid for the hit. Peterson was so tight with his money he wouldn't buy a descent suit. That left only Salvador.

The room tilted like a pinball machine. Alarm bells and all. The caffeine in my bloodstream turned to nitroglycerine, ready to explode with any beat of my heart.

"You sure you don't want that orange juice?" Mrs. Vallinski asked me. "You're lookin' a little pale."

A bit dizzy, too. I fought the spin. "You've been a great help, ma'am."

"I don't hate you as much as I thought I did, young man." She smiled, probably the first time since Martin died.

Coming here wasn't a bad thing after all. "I've got to go now."

"What's the rush? Have some juice."

"I need to find Martin's cell phone."

And when I did, I was sure to learn that stored phone number belonged to Salvador.

Chapter Twelve

UNDER THE WAN GLOW of streetlamps, my Harley roared through traffic on Northbound I-25. I cut left and right from lane to lane, tailgated ass-draggers, and squeezed between cars California style. If I was still a cop I'd give myself a ticket. But I couldn't get back to the Star Bar fast enough. My headquarters.

Considering the fiasco I'd walked in on back at the station earlier, tits and ass included, I decided not to drop in to see Salvador. I'd phone him, set up a meet, and grill him about the cell phone. If he was smart, he'd swear he'd never seen it, and then fling it into the Platte River first chance he got.

Blasting along, the Harley vibrated like a pissed off Diamondback rattler. The night air bit at my ears and made my eyes water behind Arnold's

Terminator shades. Okay, it was difficult to see wearing sunglasses at night, but it was cool. In fact, dressed in a leather jacket and boots and fingerless gloves, and with my hair whipping about in the wind, the *cool factor meter* on my ego pegged into the *Easy Rider* zone.

I leaned back, straightened my arms, and rested my feet on the highway pegs. Maria and I had spent a hundred hours cruising the Rocky Mountains on this Harley. I'd lean back like now and settle into her embrace, leather against leather, and we'd lean into the curves, riding as one body, one mind, one soul. The growl from the pipes reverberated off the canyon walls like thunderclaps, so loud we couldn't have heard a word even if we wanted to speak to each other.

But now I rode alone like Johnny Blaze in *Ghost Rider*, and though I hadn't sold my soul to the devil, I would, if that's what it would take to find justice for Maria.

I made the Star in record time, jamming down gears on 21st and Market and leaning the bike hard left into the alley. Cats scattered and roosting pigeons flew every-which-way. At the chain-link fence guarding the Dumpster, I braked hard, dropped the kickstand, and shut off the engine. My ears were ringing.

Porky stood at the open back door, smoking a Cuban cigar. I should arrest him for owning contraband, but expensive stogies made him a classier dive bar bartender. "What's your hurry, Jack?"

I got off the bike, my butt tingling and fingers twitching. "I need a drink."

"I'll be right with you." Porky moved back, blowing smoke out the door.

I stepped inside and walked past a smelly trashcan and stacked boxes of beer bottles. An old space heater hung from the ceiling, the kind usually found in auto repair shops, totally un-classy as the rest of the place.

Right off, I spotted Danny sitting at the bar, on my barstool, his grimy elbows all over Maria's sacred inscription. The fucker had a lot of nerve. I bulled my way toward him.

His buddy sitting next to him spotted me. "Trouble, nine o'clock."

Danny swiveled to face me. His cheeks turned a freaky shade of white. "Now, Jack, don't get all bent out of whack."

"Whack, Jack," his buddy chanted.

Danny snorted out a laugh, ever the comedian, too dumb to bail and run.

I reared back my right fist to knock him into next Tuesday. A meaty hand grabbed my wrist.

My cop training kicked in. Pivot. Backstep. Drop. The maneuver should've pulled my assailant off his feet. He should've hit the ground where I could kick his teeth in, but the lunk didn't budge. I came up with a left roundhouse and saw the cigar and sideburns. Porky.

"Whoa there, Jack."

I unwound like a broken garage door spring. "What are you doing sneaking up on me?"

Porky let go of my wrist. "Something's got you all fired up. Don't take it out on these boys."

I shook my fist. "He's in my seat."

"Ever think of asking him to move?"

There was a time I might have, before Maria was killed. Before her father landed on the top of my shit list. But tonight I answered the question honestly. "Why should I?"

By now Danny got it figured out and hightailed it off my barstool. "It's all yours, Jack."

His lamebrain buddy was stuck on his own joke. "Whack, Jack." He cackled. "Whack, Jack."

"More like whacko Jack," Danny said.

"Whacko, Jacko. Whacko, Jacko."

I needed to find a better place for my headquarters.

Porky said, "Okay boys, cool your jets," then turned to me, "Sit down. Tell me what's stuck up your ass."

I rubbed the burn from my wrist, surprised at Porky's Vise-Grip grip. "Vallinski's cell phone is missing." I sat on my barstool and swiped Danny's greasy aura from Maria's carved name. "I think Salvador's got it."

Porky moved behind the bar. "Tampering with evidence? That's serious shit."

"All this time I thought it was Peterson's specialty. Now I'm not so sure." I glanced at Danny and his buddy playing diddly-fuck-around at a table in the back, all slap-happy on whacko-Jacko jokes. Porky was wrong; *I'm not going to end up like those fools.*

"Ask Mina about it." Porky slid a folded cell phone at me.

I about croaked. "This it? Vallinski's cell

phone?"

"No. It's yours. Disposable and untraceable."

"You bought us cell phones?"

"You gotta stay in touch with your angels, Jack."

Angels? Charlie's Angels, aka, Jack Sabre's Angels. "Are you shittin' me?"

"Helen's idea. Protects your identity in case someone starts snooping into your phone records. They've sent many a criminal to prison."

"We're not criminals." I flipped open the phone, pulled up the call list: *Helen – Angel #1. Mina – Angel #2.*

Charlie had three.

I punched #2. This time of night, Mina Finetree was probably in her robe and curlers.

Two rings and she was on. "Don't tell me," she breathed. "You're at the Star and Porky just gave you your new cell phone, and you couldn't wait until tomorrow to call me."

"You should be a detective."

"I am now."

"Then maybe you can tell me what happened to Vallinski's cell phone."

"Cell phone?"

The tone in her voice told me she didn't have a clue. "Vallinski's mother said he had a cell phone on him when he left the house."

"I didn't see one."

"Somebody has to know where it is. Ask around the station—"

"No, Jack. I'm not saying a word about this case. I don't know anything. If I see something, I'll tell you. But I don't ask."

That was stupid of me to even suggest. Someone in the precinct would be quick to figure she was in cahoots with me. And I was off limits. Bad news. "Then snoop. Eavesdrop. I need to know who got to Vallinski's body first, before the coroner discovered the envelope full of cash."

"There were a dozen cops from three agencies at the shooting scene. Paramedics. Hospital. Morgue. Coroner's office. Anyone could have taken the cell phone. Or it's in an evidence locker somewhere logged in wrong. Misplaced. Happens all the time."

I refused to admit there wasn't something more sinister going on. "I need that cell phone, Mina."

"Go home. You're no good to us dumb on your feet."

"And while you're at it, tell Helen to find out who goes by the street name of Boss...and get me the original DNA report on the skin found under Maria's fingernails."

"You want me to find Jimmy Hofa's body while I'm at it? You know the crime lab is locked up tight."

"Find a way. That's what detectives do."

"Goodnight, Jack."

I snapped shut the phone. *Amateur.*

"No luck?" Porky asked, wiping down the bar.

"She's no help."

"Give her time. She's a smart girl." He grinned. "And pretty."

I needed *pretty* like I needed a dick ring.

Danny and his booze buddy were cutting up like a couple college boys on Spring Break, still whooping and hollering over whacko Jacko jokes.

I clenched my fist, thought about going over to their table and bashing a chair over their heads, but the bottle of Old Crow on the back bar shelf stopped me. I gave it a love stare. In thirty minutes I could be drunk enough to not give a damn about them or the cell phone.

"Forget it, Jack," Porky said.

He must've seen the want in my eyes. I swallowed and forced my mind back on track.

In the detective business, a lot of case-solving came down to luck and gut instinct. My gut told me Salvador knew about the cell phone. He took it to hide the fact that he was the last one to call Vallinski, and I'd bet the nails in my coffin he'd deny any knowledge of its existence.

I pocketed the disposable cell, pulled out my own, the one with the camera I'd never used and Salvador's phone number in speed-dial under *Dad*. Okay, Salvador was Maria's dad, but I called him dad, too.

The phone rang and rang. I figured he was trying to decide whether or not to answer the call. He probably thought I was drunk and calling to bug him about getting my badge back. Even I couldn't hide from caller ID.

"Hello, Jack."

I heard defeat in his voice. "I wouldn't bother you if it wasn't important. It's about Vallinski—"

"I told you to stay out of it, Jack. You don't know what you're dealing with."

"Where is his cell phone?"

The line grew quiet. I expected as much. His mind must have been scrambling for an evasive answer, his balls scrunching up in fear of being crushed under my boot-heel. I let him suffer through it, mull it over, decide. The first one to speak loses.

He knew it. I knew it.

I touched Maria's name carved in the bartop, told her everything would be all right. Black Jack was on the case. She could rest soon. So could I.

"What cell phone?" he whispered.

You lose. "Mrs. Vallinski told me Martin had it on him when he left the house." Bet he hadn't seen that coming.

Click. The line went dead.

I grimaced at Porky. "The fucker hung up on me."

"You must've hit a nerve."

"When I get my hands on him, I'm going to hit more than that...with my fists." I stashed the phone and climbed off the barstool, intent on riding the Harley to his house and beating the crap out of him. And I would have too, if the cell phone hadn't chirped from my pocket.

"Now what?" I dug the phone back out, read the display. *Dad.* I answered, "You damn well better not ever hang up—"

"You stupid son of a bitch, Jack. I'm living under a goddamn microscope here. They've got a bug on me, my phone, my house. The bastards know everything I do, everything I say. I can't even take a dump without them hearing me flush. Now the bastards know about Vallinski's cell phone. You and your big fucking mouth, Jack. We're dead now, damn it. Dead."

"Who the hell—?"

Click.

"Fuck." I almost threw the phone across the bar.

"Call him back," Porky said.

"Some bad shit going down. I've got to get over there."

The phone rang again. I answered, hissing through my teeth, "Christ, are you kidding me?"

"Listen, Jack. And listen good. I may only have one chance to say this."

"How can your shit be bugged? You're a cop. You have electronic—"

"Shut up and listen, damn it."

"If your phone's bugged, why would you use it? Why would you say a word?"

"The monkey is out of the cage, thanks to you. Now it's a matter of life and death. I don't give a fuck if they hear what I have to say."

"Then tell me who made the last call on the cell phone."

"I can't. You'll take it the wrong way."

"It's evidence in my investigation."

"There is no investigation. You're not a cop anymore."

"I think you had something to do with Maria's murder." There, I'd said it.

"Not me. How dare you? I tried to keep a lid on this case, undercover, low profile, until we could find out who was behind Maria's murder. I hoped her death would be the end of it, but now they're gonna kill me, they're gonna kill you, they'll kill anyone who knows about that phone."

My heart about stopped. *Anyone? Porky? Mina Finetree?* "Who's going to kill us?"

"If I knew they'd be in jail by now."

That made sense, but not the bugs. "Why can't you trace the buggers, sweep your house?"

"It sweeps clean. We don't know how they're doing it, remote, satellite maybe."

"Government shit?" I slumped back on the barstool. "The cell phone is the key."

"I'll give it to you, but it's a lit stick of dynamite. It could get you killed."

"Let me worry about that. I'm on my way."

"No. The bastards could be headed over here right now."

I imagined black SUVs pulling up to the curb, assassins piling out, ninja-looking fuckers armed with AKs and Uzis, all looking to kill Salvador...

"You've got your own muscle on the force. Call in SWAT. Get some backup, for Christsake. Take a stand."

"And risk more lives? Wise up, Jack. The fewer people who know about this the better. Meet me at the place where Maria went to swing when she was a little girl."

The memory came back like a favorite old movie. Candlelight and wine, during one of our heart-to-hearts, she'd told me her dad would take her to Observatory Park to swing on the swing-set and climb on the jungle-gym. And when she was a teenager she'd go there to read romance paperbacks and think about stuff.

"You know the place?" Salvador asked, dashing my trip down memory lane.

"Bad idea. They might follow you."

"They don't have a tail on me."

"How do you know—?"

"I'm a cop. I know."

Of course. He'd probably done some counterintelligence of his own. I would have.

"I've got to get moving," he said. "Watch your back."

"I always watch my back."

"Be there in thirty minutes."

Click.

"Thirty minutes." I looked at Porky. "I've got to ride again."

Porky scratched his sideburns. "I bet you're glad I didn't let you have a drink or two or ten, like usual."

The jury was out on that one.

I started to fold the phone, but the flashing display stopped me. *Call Ended: 1 min. 51 sec.* How could I have been so stupid to think Salvador was anything but a victim in all this? My grief over Maria had blindfolded my better judgment. That was why Peterson didn't want me on the case. Why the captain told me to stay out of it. Now that I finally understood, it was probably too late. I'd signed Salvador's death warrant. He loved Maria, but he couldn't protect her any better than I could.

I was in this cesspool up to my gonads. The only way out, get that cell phone. Get the number. Get the name. Get the bad guys. There was no doubt they'd kill for the phone because it was proof of their complicity. And they hadn't known it existed until I opened my big mouth.

I could fuck up a wet dream.

The display went dark. I closed my phone and pointed at Porky. "Forget what I told you about that missing cell phone."

"What cell phone?"

I propped my foot on the barstool next to me and checked the snubbie in my ankle holster. All secure. With good luck on my side, I wouldn't need the gun, but based on my current run of bad luck, I'd probably need all six bullets before this night was over.

Chapter Thirteen

THIRTY MINUTES WASN'T much time to jump back on I-25 Southbound, get off at the University Boulevard exit, and negotiate the neighborhood east of DU to Observatory Park. Worse, the Harley was running low on gas.

Once I got my hands on that cell phone, things were going to get dicey. Unknown forces would be on my ass, all with one thing on their minds. My murder.

I idled up to the curb on Fillmore Street. A tall lamppost stood among the trees, cast branchy shadows across the playground, and eerily illuminated monkey-bar arches and a four-seater swing-set. I recognized the Jeep I'd pulled up behind. Salvador's Liberty. No sign of him, though.

I dropped the kickstand and shut off the

engine. He had to have heard me roll up.

Bright headlights and the squeal of tires on asphalt made me look down Fillmore Street. Some lunatic was speeding away, busting the limit in a residential zone. Careless driving. Reckless driving. Being stupid. I'd have a field day writing tickets for that clown. If I was still a cop.

The car careened around the corner onto eastbound Evans. Streetlights flashed off a shiny black Lincoln, like the one in the rail yard, the night of my beatdown. A paralyzing chill clawed up my backbone. Salvador's whereabouts became a sudden and desperate concern burning a hole in my chest. Had Michelin Man and Sasquatch nabbed him? Or worse? Killed him?

I jumped off the bike. "Salvador!"

Nothing.

I ran across the grass toward the playground.

"Salvador!"

Porch lights lit up down the block.

"Can you hear me?"

A moan. From my left. By the swings. A gagging sound.

I veered toward it, running on adrenaline,

faster and faster until I plowed across a woody mulch pit toward a heap lying under a canted swing seat.

"Dad." I dropped to my knees next to him, my brain trying to register what my eyes strained to gather in the diffused light. The swing chain was wrapped around his neck, tight enough to squeeze blood from his right ear. His right eye was popped out of its socket, and his nose was laid up against his left cheek. There was so much blood he didn't look real. I would have upchucked if I wasn't so pissed off.

I loosened the chain, unwound it from his neck, and flung it aside. The links had dug angry gouges in his skin. I let him settle on his back and held his head. His hands were behind him, possibly tied. He gurgled gasping breaths. His left eye swiveled to me.

"Jack..." he muttered.

"They followed you here? I told you—"

"They..." he coughed, "...were waiting."

"Waiting? Who would have known about this place?"

"They...got...the phone," he managed to rasp through a crushed larynx. Blood outlined the edges of his teeth, burbled past his lips, leaked from his nose. He wheezed. "Jack—"

"Don't talk." He was going to be all right, just a bad beating. His left eye stared at me. I resisted the urge to push his right eyeball back into place. It stared at his jacket...at blood blossoms, growing, three bullet holes that I could see. That changed things. I doubted he'd hold on much longer. I had to press him. "Who made the last call?"

"I...did."

I fell back on my haunches. My jaw felt boat-anchor heavy. "You paid Vallinski ten grand?"

Salvador managed a grunt. The hanging eyeball swayed.

"A down payment for a hit?"

He hacked up blood.

"On who?"

He went limp.

"No, goddamn it." I shook his shoulder. "Don't die on me now!"

His last breath came out garbled.

"Fuck!"

Sirens wailed in the distance. A neighbor

must've heard the gunshots and called 9-1-1. I could see it now, Peterson's arrival, his accusatory finger jabbing at me. Salvador was dead. If I hadn't stuck my nose into the investigation, he would still be alive.

Now the heat would be on me, blast-furnace hot.

And I didn't have any answers. Just more questions. If Salvador made the last call to Vallinski, then why did these thugs need the cell phone? They hadn't followed Salvador here. They'd been waiting. How did they know where Maria went to swing when she was a kid?

Somebody who'd been close to her. Ex-boyfriend close? Family close?

The irony of his extricated eye being similar to Maria's hadn't gone unnoticed. Father and daughter had suffered the same injury. She'd lost her eye when she was a teenager. We hadn't talked about it much; it was a sore spot with her, but considering the murderer knew about this park, it seemed reasonable that he knew her when she was young.

Maybe he had something to do with her losing her eye, as well. Could be his trademark, his calling card, his own sick obsession. To see if the two MOs were connected, I'd need to find out how Maria had lost her eye.

Sirens bore down on Observatory Park. I thought about getting the hell out of there, but I couldn't leave him like that, lying in the mulch, alone. I'd sooner face a dozen Petersons than live with the fact that I'd ran.

I took off my leather jacket and laid it over Salvador's head. Fuck contaminating the crime scene. He was my father-in-law. I called him Dad, Captain, and sir on occasion. Since Maria's death, I'd called him a few other choice words...

Emergency lights strobed through the trees. A cruiser skidded up behind my Harley. Another blocked the intersection of Fillmore and Warren. Two more came in from the north. Spotlights found me.

"Show me your hands," came out a cop car speaker.

I stood with my hands in the air like the bad guy in an old gangster movie, everything black and white around me. "Call an ambulance. He's been shot." It was too late for him, but anything was worth a try. Maybe paramedics could bring him back.

A Crown Vic screeched to a stop beside Salvador's Jeep Liberty. Peterson got out, clearly visible under the streetlamp. Hair mussed. Cheap suit coat unbuttoned. No tie. He must've been called out of bed. That bothered me. How did he know there was a homicide here? And why so many cops for a 9-1-1 call?

Peterson ogled my Harley then started in my direction, but a uniformed officer intercepted him, and he stopped to talk.

A Denver Paramedics van screamed up, white with orange stripes, lights blazing. They couldn't have gotten here faster if the President was shot. Something wasn't right...

Two EMTs jumped out, and lugging their equipment, ran to Salvador lying in the scuffed woodchips under the swing set. A place that had brought him so much joy, pushing his daughter on the swing, had now become the scene of his death. How fucked up was that?

I moved across the sidewalk to the monkey-bars in the adjacent pit, leaned against the rungs, and fought to maintain my composure. What I wouldn't do for a drink right now.

The park transformed into a maze of crime scene tape and crawled with investigators. Flood lights were brought in. Generators thrummed the night air. News vans with their satellite-dish headdresses converged like vultures to carrion, all kept at bay by beat cops with stern faces.

Peterson stood near the corpse. A paramedic said something to him. He shook his head. The paramedic handed him my leather jacket. He held it out in front of him by one finger and headed toward me. The look on his face caged disgust and contempt. I was in no mood to be on the receiving end of his shit again.

"Rough night," he said, surprising me with his more cordial, sympathetic tone.

"I've had better."

"Here's your jacket."

A dark swath of dry blood stained the lining.

"Next time, don't touch my crime scene."

I slipped into the bloody jacket. After all, it was Maria's dad's blood. My dad's, in a way, Dad #2. I hoped he wasn't the bad guy I'd thought he was. Guilt pinched my stomach for even thinking he had something to do with her death. Still, he'd made the call to Vallinski. He'd wanted someone killed. His hands weren't squeaky clean.

"What happened?" Peterson asked real professional like.

"If I'd gotten here one minute sooner, the outcome might have been different."

"Yeah. We might have two bodies instead of one." Peterson looked back to the lighted crime scene. "What were you two doing here anyway?"

Honesty would only get me into a deeper shit bath. "He had something to tell me." Which wasn't entirely a lie. He'd told me he'd made the last call to Vallinski. But I wasn't going to mention the cell phone. There was something else on it the killers wanted. And now they had it. I'd probably never know what was so important that justified killing Salvador.

"What did he tell you?" Peterson pressed.

"He was dead when I got here." A lie.

"Why did you meet here?"

"Because his phone is bugged."

He angled his shoulder toward me, glanced back at the crime scene then came out with, "Any idea who might be watching him?"

"It's your investigation. You tell me."

"Look, Jack—"

"No, you look, Benny. I'm sick of your pussy-footing around."

"I'm asking for your advice, unofficially, mind you. We were almost there. That close..." He pinched his thumb and first finger together. "...to a connection between Vallinski and Mayor Hodges."

"Hodges? You're way off. Try Ray Davis."

Peterson scrunched up his face. "He's running for mayor. Why would he be involved in this?"

"He's got something on Hodges."

"Says who?"

I almost said, "Says his daughter," but stopped myself. I didn't want to give him any reason to haul her in for questioning. "I think Maria had some dirt on Davis, I don't know what, and he wanted her out of the way. I think Salvador got too close—"

"God dammit, Jack. Nobody gives a damn what you think. What can you prove?"

"I'm working this case with my hands tied to my nuts. I need my badge back."

"That's not going to happen, not until

you're cleared through Internal Affairs and the District Attorney's office. We've got rules against cops who shoot first and ask questions later."

"It was self defense."

"Give me what you've got on Davis. I'll run with it."

I decided not to tell him about the black Lincoln that sped from the scene. According to Helen, Johnny Harman had driven that car to the railroad yard when he wanted to have a little talk with me. The campaign manager for Ray Davis, the guy gunning for her dad's job, was on the top of my shit-kicking list. "I've got nothing." I lied again.

"If you get something, let me know." Peterson turned back to his crime scene.

"One more thing," I said, stopping him. "How is it you got here so fast?"

He turned to face me. "I got a call. Let's leave it at that for now."

"Bullshit."

He took a breath. "My sister, all right?"

"The donut shop lady..." Salvador was fucking her. He called her after he talked to me. No. His phone was bugged. So he stopped to see her, told her where he was going, and concerned as she was for his safety, she told her brother, the cop. No. She called the bad guys first, told them, then called her brother to throw suspicion off her.

"I don't want her name mixed up in this," Peterson said. "So keep her out of it."

"Yeah, sure." Another lie. She was more mixed up in this mess than chocolate chips in cookie dough.

He walked off.

I didn't feel bad about lying to him. Fuck George Washington and his cherry tree. I wasn't about to give up Harman. If I could connect him to Lila Peterson, Martin Vallinski, and Maria's murder, I'd nail that bastard, clear my name, and get my badge back.

Up until now, Harman was only guilty of assault and battery on a citizen. Namely me. But if he was driving that getaway car tonight, if he was even riding in the back seat, he was guilty of accessory to Murder One. Of a police officer, no less.

That would get him a needle in the arm.

Chapter Fourteen

BACK ON MY HARLEY and roaring northbound on I-25, I headed for home and some much needed sleep. Midnight had passed by the time the coroner removed Salvador's body from the crime scene. I'd stayed for that. Out of respect.

Now I could hardly keep my eyes open.

After processing everything that had happened, I began to think I should have stuck with working on cars instead of becoming a cop. The thought of greasy hands and inhaling exhaust fumes seemed comforting compared to the gore and death and heartache of police work. I'd probably still be married to Karen, hell, we might even have had a couple kids by now.

Blasting down a highway nearly devoid of traffic, I realized that all I had left of Salvador and Maria were memories. Salvador's the freshest. Our last conversation about a missing cell phone, how badly I wanted it to prove he'd hired Vallinski to kill someone. And he had, though he'd died before he could tell me who, and why.

If only he could've told me over the phone. He might still be alive. Then again, those murderous bastards listening in on their bugging devices would have probably killed him in his sleep tonight. And they'd want me dead too, now that I knew there was a cell phone. Salvador was right; anyone who knew about that phone was in danger.

If not for Mrs. Vallinski, I wouldn't have known...

A jolt of adrenaline tore into me like a pit bull. Mrs. Vallinski. I'd mentioned her name to Salvador, on his phone, on his bugged phone. Son of a bitch. They knew.

I slammed on the brakes. The Harley skidded and fishtailed, but I kept the shiny side up and flipped a u-turn on the highway, going south in the northbound lanes. I'd just passed the 6th Avenue exit where I needed to get off to get to her house. Roaring against traffic, even light as it was, I wished I had emergency lights and siren, and a badge to back me up. I stayed to the right of the fast lane, blasting along the crash wall. Several cars screamed by. Drivers honked at me like I didn't know what I was doing.

Once I cleared the viaduct where 6th Avenue ran east and west above I-25, I gauged the oncoming traffic and whipped a left across all the lanes and thundered onto the eastbound exit ramp.

Full throttle to Santa Fe. A sharp left three blocks to 9th Avenue and a hard right on Galapago. I roared up over the curb and braked on the narrow patch of front yard grass, laid the bike on its left side, still running, and dashed up the porch steps where I tripped over a body.

The house was dark, porch light off, but I could tell it wasn't Mrs. Vallinski's body. Too big. Too fat. The next door neighbor I guessed from his size. He must've heard a disturbance, and ever vigilant, he'd come to investigate, only to be ambushed for his efforts.

The front door hung wide open. Point of the bad guy's attack or escape, I wasn't sure. I stooped to the body, checked his neck for a pulse.

Nothing.

My pulse was thrumming nuclear. Angry adrenaline made a wicked brew in my bloodstream. Crouched as I was, with my back to the door, I noticed the street through the porch rails. Two houses down, a black Lincoln was parked...

Fuck! I should've scoped out the area first, before I rode in like John Wayne—

The cold steel of a gun barrel poked the back of my neck. I froze.

"Jack Sabre," a voice said behind me. "How good of you to stop by." The voice sounded like Peterson's, all right, but this time I knew better. Johnny Harman, aka Sasquatch. Damn, How'd I let him get the drop on me? Tired, emotionally wrung out, I wasn't on my best game.

I raised my hands, hoping he hadn't noticed my ankle gun. "You better not have hurt the old lady."

"Get up."

I stood, real slow and easy. The thought of Mrs. Vallinski somewhere in that house lying in a pool of blood made it difficult to keep my cool. "You've got the cell phone. What more do you want?"

Footsteps, coming around. I dared a look left, spotted Michelin Man, his face so white that even in the dim light I could see pockmarks and a scar across his cheek. He had looked better in a ski mask. But if I thought his face was ugly, his mood was even uglier. He slammed a left fist to my midsection, buckling me over, the breath knocked from my lungs.

I couldn't inhale. I couldn't see. I couldn't stand.

***

"Where is it?" An angry voice reached out of the gloom. "Where is it?" A fist slugged my face. The sickening jolt bashed my teeth together. Brain fog swirled into consciousness. Pain scattered inside my skull like startled crows. My eyesight came back, focused on crosses in front of me. Crosses on a wall. Mrs. Vallinski's wall. My stomach felt like I'd eaten a cinder block.

"I'll kill him," the Peterson-like voice shouted.

"You'll kill him anyway." Mrs. Vallinski's voice this time, harsh and clear.

My head lolled over, like my neck was

made of soup noodles. The old woman sat in a kitchen chair to my right. Pink bra and panties. Wrinkles on wrinkles. A rope looped around her arms and the chair-back. What the fuck?

I tried to move toward her, to untie her, I guess, but I couldn't move. Even when I jerked and twisted. Hell. I was tied to a chair, too. Ropes burned my wrists. My hands tingled. An adrenaline bomb went off in my head, hot and sobering.

"Where is it?"

Michelin Man stepped into my view, blotting out pink underwear with a fist to my face, knocking my head to the other side of my body. I swear I felt my neck bones crack. "What the hell are you looking for?" I spit blood. "Where's what?"

"Martin's computer," Harman's voice said, cool as could be from somewhere behind me.

"Don't tell him, Jack," she said.

"Computer?" My scrambled brain slogged through conversations I'd had with Mrs. Vallinski. She had a computer. I remembered a laptop by her chair. But Martin used library computers to email her. I was about to relay this bit of information, but this time I stopped to think before I opened my big mouth. As long as these assholes thought a computer existed, they'd keep us alive. Once they learned the truth it would be lights out forever. I had to stall them. "I've got it. At my place. My apartment."

"Damn you, Jack," Mrs. Vallinski yelled.

"Let her go. I'll take you to it."

Michelin Man let his fist fly again, caught me on the left cheek, bashing my head into my right shoulder. I saw stars and mushroom clouds. At this rate I'd need a brain transplant.

I wrenched my spaghetti neck to get a look at Harman, felt like I was wringing out a wet rag between my shoulders. My black leather jacket hadn't faired too well either, streaked and splattered with blood. My blood.

Michelin Man reared back for another go at my face.

"Wait," Harman said, stopping him.

"One more. Come on, Boss." Michelin Man smacked an open palm with a closed fist. "I'll turn his teeth to Chiclets."

Boss? Vallinski's boss? Harman's street name? What would the campaign manager for a mayoral candidate need with a street name like Boss and a guy like Martin Vallinski on his payroll?

"Untie him."

A wisp of hope rose inside me. Yeah, untie me. One second was all I'd need to bend over and pull my snubbie. I'd drop these two fuckers faster than ducks in a penny arcade.

My arms came loose. My hands dropped.

Michelin Man yanked me to my feet.

I stagger-stepped, my pummeled brain woozy. Still, I managed to stoop down to my ankle, only to find the holster empty. Shit!

"Looking for something?"

I straightened. My eyes found Johnny Harman, a tall brute with sharp cheeks and jaw, dark eyes and wavy hair. He held my .38 as if it were a coffee cup, index finger hooked through the trigger guard. His other hand rested on Mrs. Vallinski's bare shoulder. "Get the computer. You have one hour. If I even smell any of your cop buddies, she gets it."

Michelin Man pulled a knife from behind his belt, a knife Crocodile Dundee would have been proud to show off, and pressed the tip to the side of Mrs. Vallinski's right eye socket. He grinned as if popping it out would be his pleasure.

Mrs. Vallinski glared at him and spoke to me. "D-don't come back, Jack."

I inhaled a painful breath. My stomach was a boulder. "I won't let you down, Mrs. V."

"No tricks," Harman said. "If you want to see her again, alive, that is." He tossed my gun on the table.

The arrogant SOB didn't need a weapon to maintain superiority over me. He had Mrs. Vallinski. And I didn't have a computer. Even if I did, once he got it, he'd kill us. This impasse had left me with few options.

Do or die. Now or never. Fuck or get fucked.

Michelin Man pushed me outside. I stepped over the dead neighbor.

My Harley lay on its side in the grass, front wheel pointing at the porch and turned upward as if it were praying. The engine had starved for fuel and stalled. I bent to pull the bike up on its wheels. Six hundred pounds of hog didn't lever up easily, but I was mad enough to raise the Titanic.

Michelin Man stood in the door and watched me throw a leg over the seat. I swallowed dryly. The ignition was still on. With my eyes focused on the thug, I hit the start button. The starter spun the motor, but it didn't fire. Not the first time, not on the second try either.

The mixture wasn't right. It would take the electric pump a few seconds to charge the fuel rail and push out the air.

I squeezed the clutch. My left toe found first gear on the shift lever. This had been such a damn good bike, packed with loads of fond memories of times with Maria, but now I had to let them go.

I hit the start button again. The engine exploded to life. I cranked the throttle full open and popped the clutch. The Harley lunged forward like a charging bull. Michelin Man froze in the wash of my headlight. In a split second, the bike banged up the porch steps, catapulted over the dead body, and slammed into Michelin Man's crotch, flattening him and damn near bucking me off, but I ducked low to clear the doorframe header and crashed down on Mrs. Vallinski's hardwood floor. With the throttle still cranked

Terry Wright

wide open, to Harman in the kitchen, it must've sounded like a Boeing 747 revving for takeoff in the living room.

I banked for the kitchen doorway, slightly off center to the right. The handlebars were on a collision course with the narrow doorframe. I let go just as the left grip struck wood. The right grip cleared, slamming the bike to the kitchen floor, skidding on its left side, on my left leg, my left knee jammed underneath and screaming six hundred pounds worth of pain. The front tire clipped Mrs. Vallinski's chair, sent her sliding across the kitchen. I used my right leg to kick myself free. I landed on my back as the careening bike took out the table legs, dumping my gun. I caught it on the way down, cranked my body around, and elbows locked, I swooped the barrel in an arc toward Harman's last-known position.

But he wasn't there.

Mrs. Vallinski's chair slammed into the wall. She let out a yelp. The Harley engine sputtered and died, the back wheel still spinning.

No Harman anywhere. He must've ducked down the hall and ran past the laundry room to the back door. The hinges squeaked, and the screen door banged.

I sprang to my feet. Pain shot up my left leg. I fell into a zombie shuffle, not able to straighten my knee. By the time I reached the back door, Harman had straddled the backyard fence. He dropped to the ground on the other side out of view. No way could I catch him now.

I doubled back, hobbled through the front room, out the front door, stopped on the porch. The black Lincoln was already tearing off down the street.

"Son of a bitch."

That seemed to be the saying of the night.

***

Peterson and I stood over Michelin Man sprawled on the hardwood floor. How fitting he'd died with a tire tread mark running from his crotch to his chin. I imagined how that would read on his death certificate.

Laid by a Harley.

"Jessie Regar." Peterson said. "He's a specialist out of Chicago. Got a rap sheet from here to Parker Road."

I recalled how he'd put his knife blade to

Mrs. Vallinski's eye. "Did he have an MO of plucking out eyeballs?"

"He was strictly an enforcer. A leg breaker. Assault and battery stuff."

Then Johnny Harman had the ocular-gutting fetish. I needed to find his connection to Maria.

A paramedic stepped up and squinted at my face like it was something from a freak show. "We better take you to the hospital." He reached out as if to touch my puffy jaw.

I reeled back. "No hospitals."

"You look like you need the rest."

"Nobody gets any rest in a hospital."

"Suit yourself. Let's have a look at that knee."

I plopped into Mrs. Vallinski's chair. "Just wrap it up."

The paramedic knelt in front of me and opened his box of medical supplies.

Four uniformed cops wrestled my Harley out of the kitchen. The handle bars were bent back, the front wheel looked like a pretzel, and the paint job was skinned worse than road rash on a road-killed raccoon. A tow truck waited outside.

I hoped my insurance policy was paid up to date.

The paramedic went to work with scissors on my pant leg, cutting from my ankle-holstered gun all the way up to mid thigh, exposing my knee. The kneecap had been knocked over to the outside of my leg.

"Just push it back into place," I told him, though it would hurt worse than stomping on my balls, well, maybe not worse, but still...

"If you insist." With a quick thrust, he forced my leg straight, which popped my knee cap back to the front of my knee.

It felt like a cement truck had run over my leg. Pain rifled up my spine. I wanted to scream like a girl but clenched my teeth together instead.

He wrapped my knee with a white elastic bandage. "You should have this put in a cast. Three to six weeks, followed up with physical therapy."

"It'll be all right," I hissed through bared teeth.

"Yeah, that's what they all say." He left me writhing in the chair.

Peterson walked up. "The EMTs are taking

Mrs. Vallinski in for observation. She's going to be okay. Banged up some, a bruise the size of Kansas on her leg. You'll be lucky if she doesn't sue you for running her down in her own fucking kitchen."

"It couldn't be helped."

"What were you thinking? The perp was down. Why didn't you stop?"

Because there was one more bad guy in the kitchen, but I wouldn't give that information to Peterson. I would deal with Harman in my own time. My own way.

But in the meantime, I had to appease Peterson and explain why I ended up in the kitchen. "Hogs don't stop on a dime."

Before he showed up, Mrs. Vallinski had promised me she wouldn't say anything about a second man in her house. Just the one, Jessie Regar, aka Michelin Man, some thug looking for Martin.

I'd saved her life. She was on my team now. The third Jack Sabre's Angel. Okay, not as beautiful as Helen and Mina, not as smooth-skinned either, but Mrs. V had balls, that woman, Paul Bunyan balls.

Chapter Fifteen

GALAPAGO STREET WAS LIT UP like a DUI checkpoint, flashing lights everywhere, blues and reds and yellows. The yellow lights strobed from the tow truck's lightbar. Groaning and creaking, the cable hook dragged my busted-up Harley onto the flatbed. The sight was enough to make me start drinking. Fat chance. Two hours past last call, this town was drier than a mosque.

My knee throbbed as I watched the goings-on from the porch not two steps from where the neighbor had died. Shot through the face, the coroner had said before reading me the riot act for running the poor guy over with my bike. Abuse of a corpse. Contaminating evidence. Assault and battery with a motor vehicle. Not to mention he had three dead bodies in one night, and I was present at both crime scenes. As though the deaths were my fault because I wasn't living right, he suggested I join a monastery in Italy.

I told him to go fuck himself.

In the heat of battle, shit happened.

Like an angry hornet, my secret cell phone buzzed inside my jacket. I knew it was the throwaway Porky had given me; my ringtone was *Eat at Joes*. I fished the buzzer out of my pocket. *Angel #1* showed on the display. Mina Finetree.

My throat constricted. Why the hell was she calling me at this ungodly time of night? Damn! I didn't want to tell her what happened to Salvador. He was her boss...and he was dead...shit. I answered anyway. "Mina?"

"Are you all right?" she asked.

"Nothing a drink or two or ten can't fix." I wouldn't bother her with my battered knee, wrecked Harley, or the hamburger Michelin Man had made of my face. "Why are you calling me?"

"I heard about Salvador."

"No shit, who told you?"

"Peterson. He thought I should know."

"Yeah, I'm sorry, really sorry. The bastards got to him."

"Stay right there. I'm coming to get you."

"No. I'll catch a ride home from one of the boys here."

"You can't go home, Jack. Those *bastards* know where you live."

She was right. And the killers thought I had Vallinski's computer. Talk about a white lie that turned into a great white shark...with bullets for teeth. "I'm screwed."

"You can stay with me."

Little Miss Muffet librarian...? What else could I do, live on the run like, Dr. What's-his-name? The Fugitive. Harman was the one who should have been running.

When I get my hands on him—

"Jack?"

"Yeah, I'm thinking."

The ambulance with Mrs. Vallinski on board pulled out, no lights and sirens. She'd spend the night in the hospital. For observation. She'd be safe there. It was time to take care of myself, get some sleep, god dammit, if that were possible considering the turmoil in my head and the pains in my body.

"Come on, Jack. I don't bite."

"Sure. Yeah. Come and get me." I closed

the phone.

***

A red Honda Civic pulled up. Mina Finetree. I waved off the last patrol officers who'd stayed on scene until I was safely away. The target on my back felt heavy as a neon sign flashing *kill me, kill me, kill me.*

I hobbled to the Civic. Got in. The dome light revealed an entirely different Mina Finetree. She'd let her hair down, past her shoulders, brown and fluffy, short bangs and no Clark Kent glasses. Her tan cashmere coat collar was upturned a bit, spy-chick style, and her fragrance said *fuck me, fuck me now.* No librarian, boring secretary, or Miss Prude Queen USA. The woman was a sex chameleon. I about fell back into the street.

The dome light revealed something else, me to her, and her eyes narrowed against what must've been a gory sight. "Oh my God, Jack." Her breath hitched. "What happened to you?"

I closed the door, snuffing out the dome light. "I finished last in a shit-kicking contest. Just drive."

"Put your seat belt on."

Shit! "Like this windshield could do more damage to my face."

"It's the law. And you're a cop."

"Ex-cop." I buckled up and laid my head back. Pinpricks of light bubble-popped in my peripherals. The car lurched forward.

I must've passed out, sober no less, because the next thing I knew, Mina was leaning over me in the car seat and shaking my shoulder. "We're here."

I blinked.

Out the window stood a wall of two-by-four studs, black tar paper between them, garden tools hanging on them with six penny nails, an arm's length away. To the rattle of a garage door going down, I sat up.

"Can you walk inside?" she asked.

"I'll crawl if I have to." Squeezing out between the car and the wall, I wrenched my knee. Felt like a Louisville Slugger had taken a whack at it. Home fucking run.

A whole lot of teeth gritting got me to the door, up two steps, like climbing Mount Evans, but I made it through the kitchen and another ten miles to the living room couch. I couldn't have hit it any harder if I'd skydived without a parachute.

Mina helped me out of my leather jacket, all spattered with blood on the outside, mine, and streak-stained with blood on the inside, Salvador's.

She pulled my t-shirt over my head and my boots off my feet then laid me back, resting my head on a pillow. Our eyes met and locked. "Don't go anywhere," she said and left.

I gazed at the ceiling, softly lit by small halos. On the walls, cowboys and Indians, feathers and wolves and dancing kokopelli. My knee throbbed. My bottom lip felt like a tubular tire. It was a wonder I didn't blubber when I talked.

Mina came back wearing a sheer, lacy top. I barely caught sight of the tight V of her panties as she sat on the edge of the couch. She came equipped with Red Cross cotton, Band-Aids, and a bottle of rubbing alcohol.

"This is going to sting some." She dabbed a cut over my left eye, a gash I didn't know I had, set me to scrunching up my face like I'd been slapped in the balls. But I wasn't going to scream. I wasn't going to cry out. Not Jack Sabre. Not Black Jack. But I did squirm, and I hissed through clenched teeth, "Mother fuck me."

"Oh it's not that bad," she said. "Try childbirth. Now that's pain."

She dabbed, and I winced. "You have kids?" I managed.

"One. Once. A girl."

I'd seen no hint of a child living here, no toys, no clothes, no clutter, so I feared the answer to my next question wouldn't end in happily-ever-after. "Where is she now?"

"Her name was Emily. She died eight years ago."

Way to go, Jack, open up another wound. "What happened?"

"A car accident."

Our eyes met again, sharing the pain of lost loved ones.

"I'm sorry."

"Grief is survivable, Jack."

"So I've been told." Thank you, Porky.

"But we all go on, all in different ways. Me, I bury my grief in work, you drown yours in a bottle."

I liked my way better. Numbness. "And Emily's father?"

"I killed him during childbirth," she deadpanned.

"You did not."

"I wanted to, it hurt that bad." She dabbed my lower lip, probably with more force than she had to.

My eyes watered. *It hurt that bad.* I sucked my lip between my teeth to keep it away from her.

"My husband took his grief to war, got killed in Iraq. Of all the rotten luck, I ended up alone, starting over."

I knew a guy once, he married a woman with the worst luck ever; she'd lost two previous husbands to cancer. A year later, he came down with cancer. Before he died, he told me to stay clear of women with bad luck.

"Don't make the same mistake, Jack. Let Maria go. She wouldn't want you getting killed over her death."

I released my bite on my lower lip. "Salvador warned me, her murder was bigger than us, that I should stay out of it, he didn't want me to end up dead as well. I didn't listen, and look what it's gotten me."

"I see. You're a mess."

"It's not the age, it's the mileage."

"Whatever you say, Indiana Jones." She smiled then hit me with more alcohol, more dabbing, more pain.

"I could say, *You should've seen the other guy,* but truth be told, he got away without a scratch."

"Next time you might not be so lucky. Quit while you're still breathing."

"I'm in too deep, Mina... There's no going back now. I can't stomach the thought of Salvador and Maria dying for nothing."

She leaned in close, so close I could feel her warm, minty breath on my good lip. Her nose touched my nose, just barely a tickle, and she whispered, "Make sure you don't die for nothing."

In the time it took me to take a breath, I slipped an arm around her waist, touching skin on her lower back so hot I could have been caressing sunshine with my fingertips.

Her mouth fell on mine, wet and wanting, so painful I arched my back, but I parted my lips anyway, inviting her in, begging for more.

The flat of her hand wash-boarded over my abs and slid south until her fingers slipped under the waistband of my jeans. My hand took the same course of action, diving under the back lip of her panties, over the smooth curve of her butt-cheek...

Maria, Maria, Maria. Oh God.

I stopped. A chill ran me through like a sharp spear. What the hell was I doing?

Mina's hand stopped. The kiss froze, lips still pressed together. I couldn't breathe, didn't know what to do next, what to say without sounding like a total ass.

Slowly, Mina pulled back, broke the connection, and licked her upper lip, not sexily, but nervously. "I'm so sorry, Jack."

I exhaled. "No, no. It's my fault."

"It's been a long time for me."

"Me too."

"I mean...a long time since I've wanted to kiss you, Jack."

My first thought was to say, "Funny, I never wanted to kiss you, never even imagined it, not in a million years," but I didn't say anything, just wondered how I'd missed any sign of her interest in me. I hadn't thought to look behind her Clark Kent glasses, her Miss Goody-Goody façade to see the real woman. Never wanted to, not really, I still had Maria in my heart, lying next to my soul, sleeping, waiting.

I patted Mina's butt-cheek, affectionately I hoped, and retracted my hand from her panties. My palm felt suddenly cold. I didn't want to abandon her this way, but I had to...for Maria, for her memory, for the very reason I lived.

Mina slid her fingers out from under my waistband, ran her fingertips up my chest to my face and touched my chin near the welt Michelin Man had gifted me. "Someday it will be okay, Jack, to love again."

I couldn't have imagined that day, until today.

"Get some rest." She stood, gathered up her nursing supplies and sauntered off. Damn she looked good, her slim curves and sleek lines...I had to look away.

Mina Finetree. I swallowed the taste of her lips on my tongue, minty sweet and forbidden. Why did she have to go and kiss a fucked up guy like me?

Sunrise seeped in around the window curtain.

I closed my eyes.

The doorbell rang.

Chapter Sixteen

MY EYES POPPED OPEN. It took me a second to get my bearings: Mina's house, Mina's couch, an image of Mina's body. She'd nursed me. She'd kissed me. I hurt all over.

The doorbell rang again.

Who the hell could it be this time of morning? Domino's? The paper boy? Nix-nix to both. It had to be someone delivering trouble.

I struggled to gain a sitting position. The ceiling was bright white now, and the aroma of coffee and bacon wafted through the air. A blanket slipped from my chest and fell across my lap. My jeans were draped over the armrest, the scissors-cut pant leg dangling like a loose sail. I heard voices, women's voices, chatting from the kitchen.

Confusion caterpillared up my spine. I'd fallen asleep, but for how long?

The doorbell again.

"Coming." A sing-song voice.

Mina Finetree appeared from the kitchen on a beeline for the front door, hair down, white halter top, yellow shorts, long legs, Nikes on her feet. "Good morning, Jack," she said on the fly.

"What time is it?"

She pulled open the door. "Come in. Come in."

Mrs. Vallinski stepped over the threshold, gray hair up in a bun, long flower dress, white purse locked in the crook of her arm.

Mina gave her a hug. "How are you?"

"I swear if I ever have another night like last night, I'm going to become a nun."

A chuckle from the kitchen doorway, then, "I'd pay to see that," Helen Hodges said. She stood there all decked out in blond curls, tan blazer, prudish green blouse, tan slacks, black high heels.

I was too underdressed for this gathering of mother hens.

Mrs. Vallinski zeroed in on me, the nearly naked lump on the couch. "Jack, I'm so sorry my son got you into this mess."

I clutched the blanket like Linus.

Helen said, "Martin was just the batshit on the belfry floor. Now we're going after the bats."

"They corrupted my son." Mrs. Vallinski sat next to me, stroked my hair. "We want those bastards just as much as you, Jack."

"So we're going to get evidence against them," Mina said.

"Hang their asses," Mrs. Vallinski chimed in.

"After breakfast." Mina looked at me. "You hungry, Jack?"

I was. "I could eat a car battery."

"Die Hard bacon and eggs comin' right up," Helen said and turned back to the kitchen. "Coffee, Jack?"

"Black," I said though I'd rather she brought me hard liquor, but I'd been cut off the good stuff.

Mina indicated my bum knee. "Meanwhile, we'll get you up and walking."

"That should be fun, but first...I have to pee." I pointed to my jeans. "Do you mind?"

Mrs. Vallinski picked up the tattered mess. "Let's get him on his feet, girls."

Helen emerged from the kitchen with a coffee cup and set it on the end table. She and Mina each took one of my hands and levered me off the couch onto my good leg.

The blanket fell around my ankles. This was exactly the reason my mother told me to always wear clean underwear. Who'd have guessed that advice would actually come in handy?

Applying a little weight, I tested my left leg, a woman on each arm for support. A guy could do worse. The pain wasn't too bad either. I bent the knee slightly. Wrong move. My leg felt like a trout being gutted. I elected to keep my leg straight and took a zombie-step forward. If dead people could do it, so could I. "I got it from here, ladies."

Mina and Helen let me go. With Mrs. Vallinski leading the way, I lumbered down the hall to the bathroom. She handed me my jeans. I went in and closed the door, relieved myself, and struggled into my ruined jeans, a painful feat since I had to bend my knee to do it.

Then I did the dumbest thing I could have done. I looked in the mirror. Frankenstein's monster was a beauty queen compared to me. Sometime while I slept, Mina had pasted Band-Aids on my face, so swollen and black and blue I hadn't felt them stuck to my skin: one above my eye, one below my lip. A big square on my chin, and a round one on my left cheek. If I went outside looking like this, people would start running and screaming through the streets.

"Fuckin' Harman," I whispered. "I'm going to kill you for this."

A knock on the door. "You okay in there, Jack?"

Mina. I touched my lips, the lips she had kissed, the lower lip bigger than the upper, and still she'd kissed them like they belonged to Prince Charming. I looked down my bare chest, over the bruises and knots, down to my cut up pant leg, the white bandaged knee sticking out.

"Jack?"

I needed a new pair of pants. How the hell was I going to kill Harman dressed like this?

"Jack?" Helen's voice now. "Can we get you anything?"

I leaned on the sink, choking back the words I wanted to say. "Yeah, get me Johnny

Harman. Deliver him like a pizza so I can blow his fucking brains out." Which reminded me, where was my gun? The ankle holster? I stepped to the door and yanked it open. My eyes found Mina right away. "Where's my gun?"

She pointed to Helen.

Helen lifted her pant leg. My gaze dropped to her ankle. There it was. A cringe gripped my throat. I looked up at her, then back and forth to Mina and Mrs. Vallinski. "What the fuck?"

"You can't go, Jack," Helen volunteered. "But we can."

These women were way ahead of me. "Go where?"

"The Davis rally."

"Christ. Are you nuts?" Hadn't she ever heard of security for these political things, rallies, fundraisers, hootenannies, and whatever? "You'll never get in with that gun on you."

"Mina's police, Mrs. V is already on their shit list, and they'll shoot you on sight, Jack."

"But you, Helen, you're the opposition's daughter."

"And Harman thinks he's got me in his pocket. He doesn't know I'm on your side, so he won't check me for weapons."

"And just what are you going to do, pop him when nobody's looking?"

"I'm not going in unarmed, Jack."

"The gun's only going to get you in trouble."

Helen narrowed her eyes. "You don't kill a snake by cutting off its tail. You cut off its head."

"You're forgetting something."

The women glanced at each other and shrugged.

"The snake's head has the fangs," I said like it was the punch line of a bad joke.

"We'll be watching her back." Mina pulled a gun of her own, a Glock.

Before I could say a word, Mrs. Vallinski opened her white purse and angled it so I could look inside. "Ruger 9 millimeter," she said, serious as a hangman's noose.

Helen added, "We need to know who's calling the shots, Harman or Davis himself. If we can find out without shooting anyone, all the better."

"Speak for your own self," Mrs. Vallinski said, cold as a corpse on ice.

Mina touched my shoulder. "Your angels won't let you down, Jack."

I wanted to laugh in their faces, but they had the guns. "You gals are way too into this angels business." If I didn't talk them out of this harebrained plan of theirs, I'd be digging three more graves.

Chapter Seventeen

I'D HEARD IT SAID that every plan came
about through bullshit negotiation and half-assed
compromise. That was easy for me to believe,
sitting in the back seat of Helen's Mercedes as it
sped down Colfax toward Civic Center Park.
Helen drove, Mina rode shotgun, and Mrs.
Vallinski sat at my left elbow. She wore a long
blond wig that made her look like an ugly, old
hooker. The interior smelled of perfume and
talcum powder. I was the only one without a gun.

My leg was jammed in crosswise all
crooked and spazzing, but there was no way I was
going to sit on that couch back at Mina's while
these women walked into the arena of political
corruption and murder. Their plan was simple.
They had no plan, least wise nothing they wanted
to share with me. Thus the half-assed compromise:

I could go along if I didn't bug them about the plan. Some bullshit negotiation that had turned out to be; they even made me promise to stay in the car.

Yeah, right!

Barricades on Colfax had gone up at Bannock. Helen maneuvered in behind a taxi and followed it through a right turn onto Bannock in front of the Civic Center. She stayed right and pulled into the City of Denver parking lane for official vehicles only. People were crossing back and forth in front of her, so she had to go slow.

A Yellow Cab honked and went around us.

She stopped behind a black limo. The driver, who stood by the front fender, gave her a dirty look until she hung a permit on the rearview mirror, one she was privy to because her father was the mayor. The chauffeur straightened his shoulders and resumed his vigilant stance. My so-called angels may have planned everything down to the smallest detail...except one.

Me.

Doors popped open. The women got out. I did too.

Mina grabbed my arm. "No way, Jack, you

promised."

Helen glared at me over the car roof. "Get back in the car."

"I'm not letting you girls out of my sight."

Mrs. Vallinski said, "If things go bad, you can't run."

"Who's running?" I slammed the door.

They slammed their doors, too, and grouped in front of the car. "Have it your way, Jack," Helen said. "But if cow poop hits the pasture, you're walking out on your own." They turned away like a flock of pigeons.

"Fine by me," I shouted to their backs.

The limo driver gave me a crusty look. A Metro Cab screamed by and honked. "Get out of the road, buddy."

I limped after the girls, and we melted into the crowd. A bandstand had been set up on the sidewalk facing the park where a local rock band played eardrum-busting music to draw in fans and potential voters while Davis spoke from the Greek amphitheater a half block to the east. A gauntlet of souvenir booths and food venders awaited our passing.

I noticed a minimal police presence. In the

short distance we'd moved into the park, my knee was already hobbling me. I wondered how long it would take before I wished I'd listened to them and stayed on the couch.

The music faded behind us and applause rose from a gathering around the amphitheater. I made the low wall perimeter and clung to it, resting my bad leg. The girls went ahead and stopped at the precipice of the stone steps that semicircled down into a bowl of seated spectators.

Helen waved toward the raised stage.

"People of the great City of Denver," Davis said from the podium microphone. He wore a potbellied suit coat and a ten gallon hat. "Welcome to a new beginning, a new era of city leadership where the little guy is more important than the wealthy few."

Applause.

Behind Davis, a suited man stood from a folding chair. Sasquatch. I'd recognize Harman in any dark alley. He ducked behind a row of seated dignitaries awaiting their turn at the microphone, probably to give homage to Davis.

"I'm here to tell you, folks, that Mayor Hodges' days of plundering the city coffers are numbered."

Helen was already heading down the steps toward the stage. Mina and Mrs. Vallinski stood watching from their positions, the high ground. My throat tightened as I watched them put their lives at risk for me. I should be the one in the line of fire.

"He's been robbing all you taxpayers blind," Davis proclaimed to the crowd.

Black-suited goons checked Helen's progress. One put a hand on his earpiece, said something, and then they escorted her to the steps that led up to the stage. Security stopped her there.

"My administration will turn back the tide of greed and corruption."

One thug walked up to her with a metal detecting wand. My heart almost stopped. I couldn't breathe. If they found that gun—

Harman appeared at the top of the steps and waved the security man off. He lowered the wand and backed up.

"Good people of Denver, I'm going to need your help."

Helen bounded up the steps to Harman. A

quick hug, an arm around her shoulder, he turned her toward the podium.

She was in. I could breathe again.

"I need you to vote for me and traditional American values."

How she planned on getting information about Davis escaped me. Harman wouldn't tell her anything truthful. He'd lied to her about wanting to talk to me the night I got ass-pummeled in the railroad yard.

"Let your vote for me count as a strike against corruption in our city government."

The crowd chanted, "Davis. Davis. Davis."

She took a folding chair next to Harman, behind their bullshitter of the hour, and crossed one leg over the other, real casual like.

"As we strike a blow against the evil among us."

I scanned the row of dignitaries... and spotted men on the sidelines with binoculars sweeping over the crowd, security ever vigilant. A set of high-powered lenses stopped on Mrs. Vallinski. Then another. A flurry of activity erupted below the stage, black-suited men scurrying about, rallying to a call.

"Against those who would defile our names."

Two men started running up the steps that led out of the amphitheater bowl, straight toward Mina and Mrs. Vallinski. My chest took a sharp wallop from the inside. The long blond wig hadn't fooled anyone. Two other advancing security men looked to be flanking me on the right.

Son of a bitch. They'd made me too.

I staggered and looked back to Helen. She was gone. What the hell happened to her? My attention was distracted. Was she dragged off stage? Where—? Or did she rat us out?

"And crush our movement to release their greedy-fisted hold on the decent people of this great city."

The two men grabbed Mina and Mrs. Vallinski. They didn't resist, the shock in their eyes unmistakable. I wouldn't resist either; I wouldn't make things worse. But the other two men ran past me and rushed directly to aid their comrades. The guns were quickly found. Handcuffs came out and clicked on.

"Yes, my friends, the conspirators will be made to pay for their treachery."

I pressed my back to the wall, heart jack-hammering against my ribs. Salvador was right. This was bigger than me, bigger than him, bigger than us.

"So a vote for me is a vote for change, ladies and gentlemen." He waved to the crowd like he was our savior, the lying fuckin' son of a bitch. "We're taking donations at our booth. Come by. Shake my hand. Join the movement for a better Denver."

Applause.

I was alone. My angels were gone, all three, in one mighty swoop of the Davis election machine.

Chapter Eighteen

BEATING BACK PANIC and in more pain than I dared let take control of my body, or I'd curl into a fetal ball, I hobbled back to the car. It was locked.

Damn.

The limo driver, still posted at the front fender, looked at me like I was some kind of zombie. I couldn't blame him, bandaged up like my face was, jeans cut up the pant leg damn near to my swinging stuff. I not only looked like shit, I was as desperate as a man with a knife blade in his back.

I needed help and I needed it fast. Peterson. Maybe I could call him, tell him what happened. Oh, I'd catch hell for it, all right, but I was desperate.

I pulled out my cell phone, the one with the

camera I'd never use, and that stopped me. The limo driver had a car. I'd bet the keys were hanging from the ignition. He wore a nice jacket and a chauffeur's cap, sharply pressed slacks. And better yet, I'd bet he wasn't working for the rock band performing on the bandstand. I'd bet he was with the Davis bunch.

There was one way to find out.

"Nice car," I shouted to him and shuffled to the limo's back bumper. Phone held out so he couldn't doubt my intensions, I snapped a picture of the license plate.

"Hey, buster. What the fuck you think you're doing?"

His reaction was exactly what I wanted. And just to rile him a bit more, "Too bad it's parked illegally."

"Fuck you." He started toward me, big strides, chest puffed out like Superman. "Mr. Davis can park anywhere he wants."

Bing-ga-fuckin'-go.

"Now give me that phone."

I made myself look small and weak, which wasn't hard to do. "Hey. I don't want any trouble, just a concerned citizen."

And just for good measure, I took his picture too.

The brute grabbed my phone, dropped it on the ground, and crushed it with the heel of his boot. "And I'm just a concerned employee." He laughed and turned back toward his post. Just like I figured he would.

I gave him a full-fisted-fuck-you-very-much punch to his left kidney. He arched his back, twisted around just in time to say hello to my left hook in his solar plexus. That bent him over, and pivoting on my good leg, I grabbed him by the collar and slung him headfirst into the rear fender. Left a dent the size of a Colorado cantaloupe and wobbled him a good one. His hat hit the ground. He teetered long enough for me to open the back door. I guided his fall toward the opening and booted him into the car.

An old couple saw me whack the guy and stood there gaping at me.

I bent down and picked up the hat, brushed it off. "It's okay," I said to the oldsters. "I warned him not to let me catch him drinking and driving again."

The two hustled off.

I climbed in the car and shut the door just as he was sitting up. That earned him a mouthful of knuckles.

Lights out.

Propped against the long side seat, I took off my boots, no easy task considering my banged-up knee. Shucking my jeans felt like I'd taken an axe to my left leg, and then I got him out of his jacket and slacks then pried myself into them and put on his hat. The hard part was putting him into my jeans. Got a little more up-close and personal than I'd ever admit. I dragged him out of the car and propped him on my shoulder like he was a drunk buddy.

A Yellow Cab rolled by. I stopped it. "Take him home, will yah?"

The cabbie got out and helped me stuff him in the back seat. I pulled the man's wallet out of his back pocket, well, my back pocket now, found his driver's license; he lived someplace in Aurora, and he carried about three hundred bucks in small bills. "Here's the address and the fare." I handed him the whole wallet. "Take good care of him, will ya?"

"Sure." He smiled. "Thanks, mister." He

piled in behind the wheel and drove off.

I took the chauffer's post at the front fender, hat cocked low over my eyes, left knee on fire, back straight, shoulders squared. My heart thumped like a dog scratching fleas. I wished I had a gun.

Another cab went by. The cabbie saluted me like we were equals somehow. I simply nodded.

And sure enough, out of the crowd rushed Davis, Harman, and couple other goons in long coats, escorting my girls across Bannock, no handcuffs now, but I was sure they were prodded forward with pocket-hidden guns at their backs.

I kept my head low, stepped to the back door, and opened it with a flourish. Mina's wide eyes swept toward me, but I turned away before she could see my face, as if I was scanning the area for trouble. I guessed chauffeurs did that.

Davis shoved her into the car, got in, and then Harman pushed Helen in, followed her, then one of the long-coated goons started to hoist Mrs. Vallinski inside, but she wouldn't go quietly.

"Un-hand me, you cad." She swung her purse at him. It took both goons to subdue her.

The blond wig fell on the street. I had to just stand there. Couldn't help her. Not yet, anyway.

They got her in the car. One goon went in after her, the other started around the limo to the passenger side. I shut the door and hop-sprinted to the driver's door.

Even as I climbed in, the tinted security window was whining up behind the seat. The *BulletGuard* logo slid out of the groove, and the window clunked to a stop. The glass was probably soundproof too. I had hoped to hear what was being said back there.

The other goon scrambled into the passenger seat. "Let's move it."

Seatbelt snapped, I started the engine.

Pedestrians scurried about every which way, so I eased the limo from the curb. "Where to?" I asked the goon without facing him.

"The usual," he said

"Okay." Like I knew where the fuck that was. I managed a sideways glance at him just in time to see him pull a gun from his coat pocket.

My heart kicked my breastbone.

He set the gun on the seat between us. I glanced down. A Glock. Then he added two more to the pile, my snubbie and ankle holster, and Mrs. Vallinski's Ruger. If stupid was on sale today, this guy would be at the front of the line.

The light at 14th was red. I stopped the limo. The one-way going left was barricaded for the festivities. No turn possible here. I decided to make small talk. "I see you guys found yourselves some dates."

"None of your fucking business."

"Then I guess sharing is out of the question."

That got a stiff-lipped chuckle from him.

The light turned green. I accelerated forward, looking for an opportunity to draw attention to the limo, maybe a cop car to sideswipe.

No such luck.

The light at 13th was green. I could go straight or turn right onto the one-way going west. Decisions. Decisions. At the last second, I elected to make the turn, and I whipped it fast and hard. Tires squealed. The guns on the seat slid my direction.

"Hey!" the goon shouted. "Why are you going this way?"

Foot floored on the accelerator, I faced him and grinned.

His eyes got big around. "You!" He jammed a hand under his coat.

I grabbed the Glock off the seat and pumped two shots into him. *Bang. Bang.* Force of habit, my police training and all.

He folded over and wheezed like a punctured tire. At the rate the seat was soaking up blood, I figured he'd bleed out within minutes.

In keeping with my plan to draw attention to the limo, I blew the red light at Delaware, right in front of the justice center, the courthouse, the county jail, and damned if a single cop was around to see me do it.

"What's going on up there?" came a demand from the intercom speaker. I shot a bullet through it. They'd find out soon enough.

The security window started winding down. A glance at the rearview revealed the other goon with a gun. He stuck it through the widening gap.

I jerked the steering wheel right and left, screeching tires and seesawing toward the busy intersection at Speer Boulevard.

He fired the gun. The bullet spider-webbed the windshield in front of me.

I made myself small against the driver door. Two more shots tore into the instrument cluster. Maybe he thought that would disable the car. I twisted around, one hand on the wheel, the other hand firing the Glock at the goon behind me.

He let out a yelp. His gun fell on the seat with the others, this one smeared with blood. It wouldn't take but a second for Harman to take his place at the window and start blasting away. And Davis was probably working his fat ass forward. I hoped my girls were scrambling for seatbelts because they were going to need them.

I slammed on the brakes. Tires screamed. The rear wheels lost traction, careening the limo sideways to a gut-wrenching stop. Cars coming at me fishtailed and swerved and stopped in panic. The stretched limo blocked all four lanes. Horns honked. I jammed the shifter into park. "This ride is over, fuckers."

As the tire smoke rose around the car, I popped my seatbelt, grabbed the guns, and elbowed open the door.

Gunshots rang out from the fully opened

security window. Ricocheting bullets chased me out of the car. I pivoted on my bad leg and limped to the back door, the side windows spitting glass dust as bullets tried to get through to me.

The back door swung open. Mrs. Vallinski fell out, followed by Helen, both sprawling on the street. I hopped over them and dropped the guns on Helen's chest. "You lost something."

"Shit, Jack!"

Gun leading the way, I crawled in, keeping low on the back seat, fully prepared to take a bullet or two as I pumped lead into Harman and Davis. But what I saw stayed my trigger finger. Harman held Mina in a headlock, his human shield as he pressed his gun-barrel to the side of her head.

The other goon had crawled through the security window, his pant legs and shoe soles giving his intentions away. He was probably going to flank me from around front. I hoped Helen and Mrs. V had my back.

Davis cowered in the side seat, hands up in surrender, the chickenshit fat slob that he was. "Don't shoot."

"Let her go," I shouted at Harman.

"Back off, Jack, or she gets it."

God dammit. I should've kissed her longer and harder and made her listen to me. Now her life was in my hands. I hoped she'd fare better than Salvador. What I did in the next second would either get her killed or leave us all to fight another day. "Go easy here, boys."

Her eyes were mean slits of rage. "Shoot him, Jack, shoot him."

Chapter Nineteen

I SWALLOWED HARD. This was the Mexican standoff from hell. One mistake, one false move, one stretched nerve snapped, and we'd all live or die with our regrets.

"Sam...Sam!" the goon up front shouted.

The guy I shot was probably dead by now.

"Get out real slow, Jack," Harman said, his gun pressed to Mina's temple. "Or she'll end up like Maria and her father."

"Shut up," Davis growled.

My finger itched to pull the trigger, begged me to put a bullet between Harman's eyes, except one eye was cowardly tucked behind Mina's head. If I didn't kill him instantly, he could get off a shot or pull the trigger with a dying reflex. I couldn't take the chance.

"You heard him, Jack," Mina said, her

words edged with true grit. "He killed Maria. Shoot him."

"I didn't kill her," Harman said. "Had nothing to do with it."

I looked at him real hard, digging for the lie in his eye. The words spoken in this car could well be worth a deathbed confession, as none of us knew how many seconds we had left to live. Harman's arrogance alone wouldn't let him lie about something he'd rather brag about. So I believed him.

"If you didn't kill her, then who did?" I asked him. "That's all I want to know. You guys can run your dirty campaign, flush Denver down the toilet for all I care. Just tell me who ordered Vallinski to kill my wife."

The goon up front yelled, "Sam's in bad shape. We gotta get him to a doctor."

So the lucky fucker was still alive. I should've double tapped him twice.

Sirens wailed in the distance. *Shit.* Cops would only make this situation worse. It would quickly become a hostage crisis. News media would swarm the area. Hours of negotiations would end with SWAT and their flash-bang grenades, high-powered rifles, and high drama for the networks. These guys would die before I found out who hired the hit.

A clunk in the Limo's chassis told me the goon up front had put the transmission into drive. I was out of time.

"All right." I released the gun butt, letting the Glock swing back on my trigger finger, barrel pointed up. "I'll get out of the car real slow, but let her follow me."

"I like her just fine where she is," Harman said. "She's my insurance that you'll behave yourself, or *BANG!*" He jerked the gun.

I flinched.

"Another one bites the dust." Harman grinned. "How long before you run out of people who give a shit about you, Jack?"

The goon called out, "We gotta go, boss."

Davis dropped his hands to his knees. "Well then, Jack," he said in his pompous podium voice. "Seems that if you back off this case, your girlfriend here will get through this predicament with her head still attached."

"Talk is cheap. When do I get her back?"

"When I'm mayor."

"Not good enough. You could lose the election."

He looked at Harman. Harman nodded.

"Tomorrow night," Davis said, expanding his barrel chest. "I've got some important business then. If it goes off without a hitch, you'll find her in the railroad yard, none the worse for wear."

"I have your word?" That was like asking the devil if he ever lied, but it was worth a shot.

"If you behave yourelf. Captain Salvador didn't take this solemn advice to heart. Don't make the same mistake."

Now I knew. Davis was behind the killings, all right. He'd hired Martin Vallinski to do his dirty work, and Salvador figured it out, so he hired Vallinski to kill Davis, the guy who hired him to kill Maria. There were more twists, backstabs, and double-takes in this fucking deal than a square knot.

Davis wouldn't think twice about killing Mina Finetree. I pointed my trigger finger at him, the Glock hanging crosswise. "You hurt her, I'll come for you. There'll be no place to hide. I'll kill all your goons, all your associates, and then I'll blow your fucking head off and piss down your esophagus."

Davis laughed.

"Go ahead and laugh now, asshole, but remember one thing, when this is over, I'll be laughing last and loudest." One final look at Mina, her pinched eyes and clenched teeth, those kissable lips tight with anger, I wanted to say I was sorry, but she could probably see it on my face. I crabbed backward out of the car and slammed the door.

The limo squealed around and headed west, and then careened onto southbound Speer. Traffic was jammed up so thick on 13th the responding police cars couldn't get through, couldn't give chase.

Helen rushed up to me. "Jack, you left her in there?"

"I had no choice." I may have just abandoned the one woman in this world who understood me, who felt the same pain and grief as I did, who'd managed to nut-and-bolt her life back together. A survivor. I could only hope she'd live through this. "We have to back off or Mina dies."

The way I had it figured, Salvador had

faced the same dilemma: *back off or his daughter dies.* He didn't back off. Got them both killed. But the motive for the murders had to have been more than politics. Who would want to be mayor bad enough to kill a high-ranking cop and his daughter? Why risk life in prison? Or worse, execution. Something else was at stake for Davis, something much bigger, much more valuable... a business deal of some kind.

Mrs. Vallinski joined us in the middle of the street. "You're in the way." She indicated the traffic tie-up with a sweep of her purse.

Helen got on one side of me and Mrs. Vallinski on the other. I put my arms around their shoulders, and they helped me to the curb. I tucked the Glock under my borrowed coat and behind the belt of the borrowed slacks, and then directed our escape from the scene northward up the alley east of Fox Street.

Sirens echoed off the buildings around us.

I forced myself to put more weight on my left leg so we didn't look so pathetic: a business-class woman, a grandma, and a hobbled chauffeur now struggling east on 14th past the justice center. We made it the five blocks back to Helen's car on

Bannock.

Music screamed from the bandstand. People milled all around. Half of them looked stoned out of their minds.

I stood over the crushed remnants of my cell phone, the one with the camera I'd only used once. But once was enough to save Helen and Mrs. Vallinski, but not enough to save Mina Finetree. I could still taste her lips on my tongue and feared I'd never savor them again.

Sirens pierced the guitars and drums and screeching lyrics: *American Woman, listen what I say.*

Helen unlocked the car.

I got in back and propped my left leg across the seat. My knee burned like battery acid on an open sore. Mrs. Vallinski took shotgun. Mina's absence felt suffocating as a lungful of molasses. Helen started the engine.

A black Crown Vic and two patrol cars careened around the corner at 14th onto Bannock, against the flow of one-way traffic and heading our direction. Pedestrians scattered. Cars and cabs screeched to the gutters.

I ducked down in the seat. Helen put the

Mercedes in gear. Eased forward.

The Crown Vic skidded crossways in front of her, throwing up dust and tire smoke. She stopped. Braking abreast of each other, the patrol cars nosed up to the side of the Mercedes. She slammed her fist on the steering wheel.

Mrs. Vallinski said, "Fuck."

I saw us all going to jail on weapons charges.

Sirens wound down. Cop car doors flew open.

"Show me your hands!"

I stashed my gun under the front seat then peeked over the seat back. Peterson, his tie askew and gun drawn across his hood, aimed at our windshield. "Do it now."

What a drama queen.

Helen and Mrs. Vallinski raised their hands. I went one better, rolled down the window, and put on my innocent old-lady voice. "Don't shoot, officer. We didn't do anything wrong."

Peterson lowered his gun. "God damn it, Jack, what the fuck is going on?"

"Whatever do you mean, officer?"

"Get out of the car."

I told the girls, "Believe it or not, he's on our side."

Helen said, "Then don't say anything stupid, Jack."

"Who me?" I popped the door handle and took my time getting out, my bad leg and all, working it for any sympathy it was worth.

American Woman, mama let me be.

By the time I made it to the sidewalk, Peterson had already shoulder-holstered his gun and waved off his backup boys.

"What's with the outfit?" he asked.

The chauffeur's uniform. Crap. Add carjacking to my list of charges, and how about assault and battery. Actually, I hoped Davis's driver got home okay. But to Peterson I said. "Happy Halloween."

He frowned, unamused. "You gonna tell me what's going on here, or do I have to take you all downtown?"

My first instinct was to tell him everything, have him put out an APB for the limo, alert the State Patrol, the National Guard. Al-Qaeda. But that could get Mina killed, sure as if I'd pulled the trigger myself. So I had to deny everything. "We came to listen to the music." I pointed to the bandstand.

American Woman, hey, hey, hey a.

"The limo, Jack. I've got a chauffeur downtown claiming he was carjacked by some crazy bastard with a limp."

"Really?" I painted a dumbfounded look on my face.

"A cab driver dropped him off at the station. He's wearing your jeans, the ones the paramedics cut up last night. And you're wearing his jacket."

I could feel the handcuffs snapping around my wrists. "Give me a break, Benny."

"And then there was a problem on 13th, a limo tying up traffic. Witnesses say the driver got out on 13th and headed north with two women matching your descriptions."

"Oh that, just a little misunderstanding, is all."

"The driver had a limp."

"Look, Benny." I leaned to his ear. "I got my balls in a sling here. Don't shackle me any worse than I am."

"The department can handle it, whatever it

is. But you've gotta let us know what you've got."

"You guys had your chance. Now Salvador's dead—"

"That's exactly why you should stay out of it, Jack. You're in too deep." He poked a finger at his chest. "Emotionally."

"Just let us go, Benny. I need some time to figure this out." And I didn't need the police pulling over Davis's limo and getting Mina killed.

"Why should I?"

"They killed Maria. They killed Salvador. For God's sake, let me nail these guys."

"What guys?"

"If I tell you, they'll kill you too. Don't you get it?"

He glanced at the patrol officers with him, his wristwatch, and then back to me. "I don't know, Jack." An exhale. "An hour, maybe two."

"Come on, Benny. You can do better than that."

"All right. Tomorrow. Turn yourself in. But no more dead bodies, Jack. I'm sick of cleaning up after you."

That was the point. I had to get Mina back. Alive.

Chapter Twenty

THE DRIVE BACK to our headquarters at the Star Bar couldn't have been more sullen if we were riding in a hearse. As if Mina lay in back, in a casket, and a bugle squawked out *Taps* through the stereo speakers. The only things missing: a twenty-one-gun salute and a shovel.

Helen parked alongside the Star and shut off the Mercedes, the only car in the parking lot. "This place open?"

"Oh, yeah." I knew Porky's business hours like I knew my birthday, and I knew why the place would be dead this time of the afternoon. Most of his patrons came in for early happy hour at 7:00am and were drunk by nine. After sleeping off their stupors under a shady bridge somewhere, they'd come back for late happy hour, 6:00pm to closing. My drinking problem hadn't gotten that bad; I hadn't slept under any bridges, yet.

Mrs. Vallinski turned in her seat and lifted her purse toward me. "Can I take my gun inside?"

"Leave it in the car."

I got out, stiff-legged, and opened the door for Mrs. Vallinski. She spread an eagle getting her feet out, so I stopped her long enough to tug her dress down over her knees.

"You're such a good boy, Jack."

I took her hand and helped her to her feet. "Just don't do that around Porky. He'll have heart attack."

"Is he cute?"

"To an orangutan, maybe."

"Or a hippo." Helen led the way to the front door, which sat in an alcove under a star-shaped neon sign aglow in the shaded bar-front. I limped to the door and held it open for Helen and Mrs. Vallinski.

They stepped inside ahead of me.

"Hello there, baby," Danny crowed to Helen. He must not have gotten the memo that it was time to sleep it off under a bridge somewhere. At least he had the good sense not to occupy my barstool. "Come sit by Danny boy." He patted the seat next to him.

Helen flipped him the bird.

Porky stood by the back door, paintbrush in hand, applying the final touches of red to the word *Patio* he'd printed on the wall. The trashcan and beer bottle boxes were gone, the ratty wallpaper replaced by bright white paint, new wood paneling halfway up... "What the hell are you doing to my bar?"

He turned around. He'd shaved off his Elvis sideburns. Holy shit. Now he looked like a Mexican version of Alvin the chipmunk, all puffy cheeked. He eyed my chauffeur's jacket. "New job?"

"New patio?"

"I got the toilet fixed," he said. "Good time to upgrade... like the rest of the yuppie bars in LoDo. Who knows, maybe I'll get a better class of clientele, so no more pissing in the alley, you hear?"

Mrs. Vallinski gasped. "You peed in the alley, Jack?"

"No I didn't." *God!*

Danny waved his hand. "I did."

"You would," Helen told him and pulled a

stick chair out from under a table for Mrs. Vallinski.

She sat down. Her eyes oozed disbelief as she looked around the bar, her nose wrinkled with disgust. "This is your headquarters?"

"Headquarters?" Danny snickered.

I shot him a shut-the-fuck-up look. "Don't let the place fool you, Mrs. V. I did some of my best drinking in here." I limped to the bar and touched Maria's carved name, the only way I could say hello.

Porky set his paintbrush on the paint can at his feet. "What happened to your leg?"

"Never mind my leg. What the hell's gotten into you, changing things around here?"

Stepping forward, he outstretched his arms like a realtor showing off a prized listing to a potential buyer. "Picture it, Jack, flat screens in the corners, sports on every channel, a new pool table, dart board, video games, booths along this wall, nice leather ones—"

"Hold on there, Porky." I thought I'd puke. "You can't do that. You'll ruin the ambiance of the Star."

"Ambiance is just a fancy word for stinks,

si?"

"Stinks?"

"Gotta change with the times, Jack. Get better. Make improvements. That's good advice for you, too."

"Here, here," Helen cheered. She'd moved behind the bar to the brown-stained Mr. Coffee pot. "I agree with him, Jack."

"Whacko, Jacko," Danny chimed in.

I ignored the prick. All this bar ruining was going to cost Porky a fortune. Had he won the fucking lottery? "Where are you going to get the money for all this shit you're talking about?"

"Check came yesterday. Lower Downtown Improvement Funds. A loan from the city. *Si*? My brother-in-law and his crew are getting new furniture and TVs right now."

The walls could've collapsed in on me; I wouldn't have felt more crushed. "What's the rush?"

"I got a loan to pay back." Porky nodded to Helen like they were coconspirators in a plot to fix Jack Sabre, and then he asked me, "So your turn. What happened to your leg?"

"I dumped my bike, but that's the least of

our problems." I inhaled. Lucky me to be the one to deliver bad news. "Salvador is dead."

Porky's puffy cheeks deflated. "How?"

"They beat him half to death, and then they shot him."

"Who?"

"It gets worse. They kidnapped Mina Finetree."

"Mina?" Porky wobbled. He sat in a chair across from Mrs. Vallinski and patted his pudgy hand over his heart. "What will you do?"

"We can't do anything." Helen set a coffee mug in front of Mrs. Vallinski. "Or they'll kill her too."

"Oh we're going to do something, all right, I just don't know what." I rubbed my jaw and thought about getting a coffee for myself, spiked to the gills with Kentucky Bourbon, but I had to stay sharp, figure out what to do next to get Mina back and screw up Davis's so-called business deal.

Porky asked me, "Did you get the cell phone?"

"They got to it first, left Salvador for dead, but he lived long enough to tell me that he was the one who had made the last call to Martin

Vallinski."

"He was my son," Mrs. Vallinski said.

Danny snorted out, "Jack shot him," and got down from his barstool. "Now he's not a cop anymore."

"Mind your own business," I told him.

"Children," Porky said. "Behave yourselves. Tell me, Jack, why did Salvador call Vallinski?"

I wasn't sure, but I had a hunch that I didn't want to repeat in front of Mrs. Vallinski, that her son was hired to do another killing, so I elected to tell Porky, "I don't know."

Porky stood. "You'll figure it out, Jack." He walked back to his *Patio* paint job.

I sat in his chair, stuck my throbbing leg straight out to the side, wished Mina was with us to pamper me like she'd done last night. Then again, this close to Maria's shrine, I should have been shot for even thinking—

"Ma'am." Danny staggered to the table and stood beside Mrs. Vallinski, his hands clasped together. "I'm sorry what happened to Martin."

"You knew him?" She twisted around in the chair so she could look up at Danny. "You

Black Jack

knew my son?"

That wasn't hard to believe, two lowlifes knowing each other.

"We hung out, sometimes, at the mission."

Right again. That was how Maria crossed paths with Vallinski, at the *Jesus Saves* shelter on Park Avenue, aka The Denver Rescue Mission. She had volunteered there to help the homeless. Old news. "Go sit down, Danny."

"We got the donuts together," he said.

"Donuts?" Mrs. Vallinski asked.

"From the place on Kalamath."

I knew the donut shop. The layout. The girl working the counter. The sweet smells. And Vallinski knew the place too. And Salvador knew the owner, only too well. Lila Peterson. Detective Benny Peterson's sister. Salvador's fuck bunny. A regular family affair over there.

"You like donuts?" Mrs. V asked him.

"The boss likes donuts."

Danny was so drunk he could hardly stand still much less make any sense. I already knew Harman was the Boss, his street name, anyway. And who cared if he liked donuts? "Get out of here, Danny."

"No, let him speak," Helen said. "What kind of donuts?"

"Don't know. We went in the truck. Most every weekend. Sun wasn't even up when we loaded the boxes."

I couldn't fathom why it took two men and a truck to pick up donuts for the homeless shelter. "How many boxes, Danny?"

The fucker ignored me.

"But I'm sorry, ma'am." Danny blinked alcohol-bleary eyes at Mrs. Vallinski. "Martin wasn't a nice man. He was always mean to me, kinda like Jack here, always looking down on me, like he was better than me."

I groaned. "Everybody is better than you, Danny."

"Be nice," Mrs. Vallinski barked at me, her eyes tearing up, then to Danny, "I'm the one who's sorry, young man, the way my son treated you. Martin was a good boy, once upon a time."

"I'm not s-sorry he's dead," Danny sputtered out. "Just sorry for your loss."

I had to agree with him on this point. One less scumbag in the world, but Danny's little spark of humanity touched me some. Maybe I had been a bit rough on him...

"Get back to the donuts, Danny." Helen drummed her fingers on the scarred tabletop. "How many boxes?"

"I dunno, hundreds, I guess."

"Hundreds, Danny?" I figured he didn't know how to count that high. "Nobody gets hundreds of boxes of donuts."

"The boss did." Danny teetered on boozed-up legs. "And they were heavy boxes."

Heavy boxes? "Donuts aren't heavy."

Helen slapped her hand on my forearm, stopping me. "Danny, think real hard now, did you ever look in the boxes and see these heavy donuts?"

His face turned ashen, and he stumbled back a step. "Oh no, ma'am. We were never allowed to look in them boxes." He shook his head. "They were tied shut with brown twine, and taped too. No, those donuts were off limits, didn't matter how hungry I got loading boxes in the truck."

"You poor boy," Mrs. Vallinski said.

Heavy boxes? Tied and taped shut? I pictured the donuts inside those boxes. Square donuts. White blocks of cellophane-wrapped cocaine or heroin. Green bundles of counterfeit cash. These donuts started to fit Porky's definition of ambiance. *Stinks.*

"Where did you take the donuts, Danny?"

"The mission."

Now we were getting somewhere. Harman's headquarters. The rescue mission. Of course. The place was big enough to hide a gang of political upstarts, drug runners, and murderers. And maybe one kidnapped Mina Finetree. My brain started to wrap around a rescue mission of my own.

I levered myself to my feet. "Come on, Danny." I grabbed him by the scruff of his shirt. "You're going to get us inside your boss's headquarters."

He fluttered like a wet bird. "Let go o' me."

Helen got out of her chair. "Go easy on him, Jack."

"I know where they took Mina."

"Where?" Mrs. Vallinski asked and rose up, scraping the chair on the floor.

I was halfway to the front door. "The homeless shelter on Park Avenue. Headquarters, right, Danny?"

Danny rolled his eyeballs like I'd said something stupid. "The boss ain't there, Wacko Jacko."

I stopped, gave him a shoulder shake. "What makes you so sure?"

"Cause his headquarters is at the donut shop. Best headquarters ever. Better than this dump." He waved a grungy hand around the Star.

I grabbed his shirt front and lifted him off his feet. "You gotta be shittin' me."

"I'd never shit my favorite turd, Jacko." Danny snorted.

The donut shop. On Kalamath. Lila Peterson's pothole. Harman's headquarters? Oh, wasn't that just fuckin' honky dory.

Chapter Twenty-One

HELEN DROVE THE MERCEDES. Danny rode shotgun, head leaned against the window, soused out of his liver. Gritting my teeth, I rode in back with Mrs. Vallinski, my bad knee bent and burning. Speer to Kalamath and south to Sixth Avenue. I fished my gun out from under the front seat. If Harman and Davis had Mina holed up in the donut shop, it would take a gun battle to get her out. No problem. I was in the mood to kill some bad guys.

Lila Peterson and Captain Salvador. Their relationship. That was the puzzle. What were they up to? My best guess was a double-cross. Lila hooked up with Salvador to get information on the investigation. Salvador wanted to get closer to Harman and used Lila for intel. A little fucking on the side was like sprinkles on donut glaze. But once Davis entered the picture, the stakes got higher. And deadlier.

Helen turned into the parking lot in front of the donut shop. No shot-up limo. No black Lincoln. Just smoke. Pouring out the door seams. "Oh, shit, Jack." She jammed on the brakes.

People ran back and forth in front of the car. Bystanders clumped together on the sidewalk, mouths hanging open. A man yanked on the donut shop's front door handle. Again and again. It wouldn't budge. If Mina was in there...

"Fuck!" I scrambled out of the car, gun in hand. "Everybody get back."

Screams, horns, scampering feet: sounds faded as I lumbered toward the smoking storefront. A fire inside me raged so fierce it drove me forward, faster and faster, damaged knee and all. I raised the gun and fired at the window. Plate glass blew in. Smoke blew out. I held my breath and leaped through the opening into superheated air that slapped my face with a wicked hand. Smoke blinded me. I hit the floor hard. My knee felt shotgun blasted. I flattened out on my stomach in the cooler air below the swirling smoke and yelled, "Is anyone in here?"

I made out the curved glass display case, the swinging saloon gate to my left, and heard the breathy sound of fire muffled behind the door to the backroom. And another sound. Grunting? Someone gagged and tied up? Mina? Or was my imagination ablaze as well?

"Hello?"

I swore I heard a raspy squeal.

"Shit." Gun first, I crawled under the gate and across the floor behind the counter. Smoke spewed out from the seams of the backroom door. Oddly, the smoke smelled oily, not woody as I'd expect from a building on fire. I stole a breath and felt the door. It was hot, as I expected. I held my breath and pushed open the door, staying low in case a wall of fire blew out. I'd seen the movie *Backdraft*.

No fire, just black smoke billowed out above my head. I expected darkness, but flames illuminated the smoke in eerie shades of yellows and reds glowing like the pillars of hell. They gave me enough light to see feet lying on the floor, a rope around the ankles, bare legs, a woman's bare legs, and more smoke. "Mina!"

The legs twitched.

Son of a bitch! Harman said he wouldn't harm her. I inhaled smoke, coughed, and crawled GI-Joe-style toward her. Overhead fluorescents exploded and rained down sparks. My lungs burned. I didn't dare take another breath as I scrabbled past a square metal vat, a donut fryer, billowing fire and heat. Cceiling tiles spontaneously combusted.

I dropped my gun, grabbed the rope tied around her ankles, and back-crawled, pulling her along like a sack of flour. My knee shrieked out in pain. Or was that sound coming from my throat? With all the crackling and squealing and smoke, it could have been the devil himself screaming.

My feet hit something solid. I cranked around. A wall. A fucking wall. Where did that come from? I could've sworn I'd crawled straight in and straight back. Somehow I'd gotten turned around. I couldn't see the door; it had swung back closed. The smoke had thickened enough to nearly black out the firelight. Acrid fumes chewed at my eyeballs. I couldn't keep my eyes open. Too painful. And how much longer could I hold my breath? Seconds at best.

We were screwed. Damn!

I dragged Mina to the right, collided with table legs. Shit. Went the other way. Mina stopped me. What the hell was she doing? I yanked her harder. She wouldn't budge. "Mina!"

She didn't answer. She wasn't moving. Not a sound. What had she gotten hung up on?

I crawled over her, felt my way up her legs to her panties, across her torso to her chest, over her padded bra to her shoulder, to an outstretched arm and down to her wrist...

Metal bracelet. A chain. Jesus H. Christ. Harman had shackled her to something. She wasn't going anywhere. I couldn't leave her. We weren't going to get out of here alive.

"You bastard," I shouted. Now I had no choice. I had to inhale smoke and air hot enough to boil eggs. My next breath felt like a garden rake clawing down my throat.

I had to filter the air I breathed, but with what? The chauffer's shirt I wore was too thin. Something thicker. What? Mina's padded bra. I jammed my hand under her left bra cup and shoved my face into the soft padding. While I fought off convulsive coughing, I sucked in sweet air. The firemen would find our bodies like this and wonder what the fuck we were doing.

A crashing sound made me lurch. I thought the ceiling was coming down on us. The backroom door slammed to the floor beside me followed by the immediate chill of sprayed water.

Soaking water. Life-saving water.

I wanted to leap up for joy but kept my face buried in the bra cup. The firemen would get us out. They'd revive her.

With a thunk, an axe came down on the shackle chain. Hands grabbed my legs, started dragging me. I held on to Mina, dragged her along with me across a slick, water-soaked floor, out to the front room.

More firemen joined in, pulled me off Mina, and slapped an oxygen mask on my face. Gulping air like it was whiskey, I caught a glimpse of two men carrying Mina out. Then two firemen, one on each side of me, carried me outside.

Bright sunlight made me squint. Fire hoses snaked across the ground every-which-way. Sirens. Breaking glass.

Mina was already on a gurney and being loaded into an ambulance. A paramedic stood over her, performing CPR. Only her sooty feet were visible through the open back door, jerking every time he compressed her chest. She was worse off than I'd imagined. Harman would die for doing this to her. Slowly. Not quickly like I'd killed Martin Vallinski. He went to hell easy.

The firemen set me down at the curb, not fifteen feet from the ambulance. Water dripped from my hair.

Helen knelt next to me. "Jack. You all right?"

I was soaked, singed, and crispy creamed. Better than being dead.

Mrs. Vallinski stood behind her, clutching the purse that held the gun. Her grey lips were pinched thin, and her wrinkles seemed deeper than usual. Angry wrinkles. I had a feeling she wanted to off Harman herself.

I pulled down the oxygen mask. "She's going to be all right," I managed to rasp out, more to assure myself than anyone else. My voice box felt like it had been dug out of an Egyptian tomb. I coughed.

A fireman shoved the mask back in place. "The EMTs are a little busy now, so keep this on until they can get to you."

Danny was nowhere in sight, probably passed out in the car. He had a lot of explaining to do. Like why would Harman burn down his headquarters, for starters? But before I grilled the drunk, I'd thank him for telling us to come here. He'd saved Mina's life.

The ambulance hadn't moved. What were they waiting for? Get her to the hospital. "Check on Mina," I mumbled through the mask to Mrs. V. "See what's..." I coughed, "...taking them so long."

The feet in the ambulance kept jerking.

Helen said, "They're working on her, Jack. Give them a chance to stabilize her."

"Stabilize hell..." I hacked. Talking was more painful than it was worth.

She swiped at my forehead and cheek with a tissue. "You're a mess."

"What else is new?" I inhaled dry oxygen. My throat felt like seared meat.

A black Crown Vic careened into the lot, emergency lights winking blue, white, and red. Peterson. He stopped beside the ambulance and piled out like the seat springs were jabbing his ass.

"Just great," I muttered and hacked.

"Go easy, Jack," Helen said.

I wasn't much of a threat to him now. I'd be easy to arrest and haul off to jail. Bad knee, burned lungs, hell I couldn't even belt out a hardy fuck you.

Mina's feet stopped jerking.

Peterson poked his head into the back of the ambulance then looked at me and shook his head. What the hell did that mean? He was disgusted with me, as usual. Right? That was it. That's why he looked...sad?

My heart seized. I tried to get up. The fireman held me down. "She's not dead," I rasped. "Tell me she's not dead."

He looked at me stupidly.

"No." I shoved the fireman aside and ripped off the mask.

Helen reached out, grabbed my shirt. "Jack. Stay here."

"Try and stop me." I yanked the shirt out of her hand so hard the sopped fabric ripped.

"God dammit, Jack."

I levered myself to my feet. The fireman came at me, but I hit him with a don't-fuck-with-me glare that stopped him. Smart man. I hobbled to the ambulance door.

Peterson blocked the entrance step. "They told me what you did. You tried, Jack. You tried to save her."

"No. I did save her, dammit."

"She's gone."

I shouted at the medic, "Keep trying."

"We did everything we could."

I shouldn't have left her in that limo. Why did I think I could save her by not shooting those bastards? I was damned if I did. Damned if I didn't. Why did I hesitate? I should've killed those bastards when I had the chance.

She died anyway, damn it all to hell. She died anyway.

"Oh God no, Mina, I'm so sorry." Hot tears zapped my eyeballs. I started bawling, bawling my eyes out, bawling like a baby. A wuss, a wimp, a loser... "Mina. It's my fault."

Peterson grabbed me by the shoulders and shook me. "Jack. Stop it."

"I got her killed."

"Get hold of yourself."

"Fuck you." I raked his hands off my shoulders and shoved him backwards. Before he could rebound, I lunged up the step and into the ambulance.

"Get out of here," the medic shouted.

I fell on Mina, clutching her limp body to my chest, crying so hard I could hardly see her soot-smeared face. Her hair smelled burnt and greasy. "Mina, please forgive me."

A glint of silver caught my eye, like a flash in a pool. I blinked. Silver rings adorned her ear from top to bottom. Silver rings? I scrambled back and took a good look at her sooty face. Her left eye socket was empty. Harman's dirty work.

My stomach seized.

Medics had already flanked me, set-jawed and sure to throw me out.

"Wait."

Peterson shouted into the ambulance. "What the fuck do you think you're doing, Jack?"

"I've seen this girl before. She works the counter." An anvil could've fallen out of the sky and hit me on the head, I wouldn't have felt a thing.

"Get down from there."

I stumbled to the door, climbed down the step, looked over the scene of destruction. The donut shop roof breathed fire and exhaled a roiling column of smoke into a blue sky. Rubberneckers gathered and gawked. Fire truck engines rattled. Diesel fumes stung my nostrils. A dead girl lay behind me. Yet I felt euphoric, like the buzz I'd get from chugging Old Crow.

"Mina's not dead." It came out a whisper.

I spotted the black limo idling at the curb. The back door window was down. Harman's face stared out at me, smiling a cocky sort of shit-eating grin. He had Mina by the hair, gun to her head. We locked eyes, couldn't have been for more than a second, but in that second I promised he'd be a dead man.

I went for my gun in my waistband, but it wasn't there. I'd dropped it in the burning donut shop.

The window slid up, and the limo peeled out, speeding east on Sixth Avenue.

I started limping toward the Mercedes to give chase, but Peterson grabbed my arm, spun me around, and slapped a handcuff on my wrist. "I warned you, Jack. No more dead bodies. Now you're going to jail." He cuffed my other wrist. "And you can rot until you decide to cooperate."

I went numb.

Chapter Twenty-Two

SITTING IN JAIL wasn't so bad if I didn't count the ever-present stink of urine, the concrete slab they called a bed, or my closest companion, a stainless steel toilet. The occasional clang-clack of a steel door made me wonder if someone was coming or going. I would be staying put, according to hot-shot Benny Peterson, until I told him what he wanted to know.

Fat chance. Off the force or not, this was my bust. He'd had his chance to crack the case. Besides, *vengeance is mine, sayeth Jack Sabre.*

Clang-clack.

My throat felt raw from the smoke I'd inhaled. If not for the dead donut shop girl's bra cup, my lungs could have been damaged. I had her and Maidenform to thank for saving my life.

I sat on the butt-hard bed, wondering what

she had done to get herself killed. Maybe the same thing Maria had done. Maybe she'd found out what her boss was really cooking in the backroom at four in the morning and threatened to go to the cops, assuming Lila Peterson was in cahoots with Harman and Davis.

I assumed a lot in this line of work. Sometimes that was all I had to go on. Gut instinct.

I settled back on the slab where my wet pants had made a perfect ass print on the concrete. When I propped up my knee, the sharp pain subsided to a dull throb.

Clang-clack.

Another someone was coming or going. I wished I was going. Maybe Helen would bail me out again. Or had I exceeded my limit? At this rate, I'd have more court dates than Lindsey Lohan.

Echoing footsteps. Heavy boots. In a hall down the way somewhere.

"Hey!" someone shouted, the voice tinny and demanding. "What are you doing in here?"

Fftttt. Fftt-fftt.

The hairs on my neck porcupined. There was no mistaking the sound of a silenced handgun. I sat up, board-stiff, my heart pounding.

Bang, bang.

Service weapon, no silencer. Patrol officer, maybe a detective. Jailers didn't carry guns.

"Drop your weapon," came next.

Fftt-fftt.

A *huff* and a *thud*. "Officer down." Aoogah alarms started blaring. Paranoia lightning-flashed through my mind. Someone had breached security, and I'd bet my pension he was an assassin Harman had hired to kill me.

I hit the floor, belly first. There was no place for a rat to hide in this small cell. What else could I do but keep my head down? I was fucked.

Fftt-fftt.

A scream.

Logic crept into the paranoia. Or maybe it was denial, but killing me didn't make any sense. Harman had his leverage against me. They held Mina for insurance. Or maybe they didn't think that was enough to keep me in line. After all, they'd seen me at the donut shop. I hadn't backed off. I hadn't behaved. And they'd caught me red-handed and sooty-faced. Son of a bitch. No wonder Harman was smiling at me through the limo's back window. He had good reason to kill us both. And he was obviously in one hell of a hurry to burn me.

Clang. Clack.

The steel door at the end of the hall opened and closed. Then footsteps. Coming fast and loud.

"Jack."

I looked up. Benny Peterson. He had a goddamned gun. The traitor. I knew it.

Fftt-fftt. From down the adjoining hall.

"We don't have much time." He tossed me the gun, a Glock, no silencer.

I almost didn't catch it, shocked as I was.

"I'll get the door open," he said. "We're going out the back way." He took off.

The prisoner dock. Of course. I checked the gun clip. Full. Barrel cold. Not fired. I got to my feet. The aoogah alarm started chewing on my nerves. The entire jail complex would be on automatic lockdown. Peterson had better have a get-out-of-jail-free card.

The door buzzed. He'd made it to the control room.

I slid the barred cell door open, and peeked out, first to the right in the direction Peterson

Terry Wright

went. Nothing. Then left from the direction he had come. All clear. I was about to make a hobbling dash to the right when:

Clang-clack.

The security door at the left end of the cell block opened. The alarm got louder.

I held back.

A figure dressed in dark, baggy clothes rushed in, arms straight, elbows locked, gun sweeping side to side. He wore a mask with goggle eyes. Star Wars came to mind. He stopped at a cell and pointed his gun at the inmate inside.

"Don't shoot me, man."

He shifted to the next cell. The inmate said, "Who you lookin' for, buddy?"

"I'm not your buddy," the assassin's tinny voice said.

Fftttt.

The fucker shot the guy like a caged squirrel. I was in deep shit. What I wouldn't give for a good leg right now, but if I made a run for it, he'd mow me down for sure. However, I had one thing he wouldn't expect. A gun of my own. Thanks to Peterson.

I eased the barred door closed but didn't let

it latch, and then slouched back, gun extended and shaking some.

Finger on the trigger. My breath held steady.

Where the fuck was Peterson? The control room was at the other end of the hall. He had to see this fucker stalking up to my cell. Maybe lockdown was keeping him locked out.

I was on my own.

With my luck, I'd spray bullets at the assassin, but they'd ricochet off the cell bars. Better if a deputy plugged him, but they were probably downstairs in the armory getting their guns. And bulletproof vests.

I didn't have the luxury of waiting for the deputies to do their jobs. Surprise was my only option. But where was the shooter now? I leaned forward, stole a glance, jerked back. Two cells down, still coming. Methodical in his search. And one thing worse. His baggy clothing looked like body armor. Head to toe. I was about to become the new guy at Crown Hill Cemetery.

He was close enough now that I could hear the leather in his boots squeak. I'd have to aim high, shoot for the face, so I took a standing position, a firing range pose. My knee burned and my trigger finger twitched. Where the fuck was Peterson? Where were the deputies? I swallowed sand.

The assassin must've noticed my cell door unlatched. He didn't just slink into my sights. He jumped in front of me, gorilla style, his gun as big as a cannon in my face. It startled me so bad I yanked the trigger.

Bang.

He didn't even flinch. "Nothing personal, Jack." The words came out all raspy through a speaker in the mask.

Instinct dropped me to the floor at the same instant he fired. I angled my gun upward, shot two bursts at a time. Real fast. *Bang, Bang. Bang, Bang.*

Hit him dead nuts in his groin.

The body armor kept the bullets from going into him, but the impacts buckled him over like a kid in a schoolyard fight, cupping his balls as if they were on fire.

That gave me a second to slide open the cell door and bull him over. He landed on his back, squealing like a pig. I straddled him and shoved the Glock against his left goggle lens. "Nothing personal, fuckhead."

I pulled the trigger. Blood back-splattered out the bullet hole then gurgled out the goggle lens. At least he'd stopped squealing. I couldn't say the same for that goddamned alarm.

Footsteps rushed up behind me. I swiveled the gun around. Peterson.

"Let's go. SWAT is on the way."

What was he talking about? Go where? "The guy's dead."

"Come on, Jack. I don't have time to argue with you."

He was talking about a jailbreak? "Are you nuts?"

"This guy failed to kill you. The next guy might succeed. You're not safe as long as they know where you are."

Now *that* I believed. I climbed off the bad guy, probably a Chicago hit man. Good hired help was hard to find these days. The Glock went behind my waistband.

Peterson led the way back down the hall and through a door he'd propped open to the control room. Sci-fi like high tech stuff surrounded me, video monitors stacked floor to ceiling, keyboards and consoles, bulletproof glass with a three hundred sixty degree view. Nobody around. "Where are the guards?"

Peterson typed on a keyboard. "When the shooting started, they headed for the armory. I had to figure this shit out myself." He swiped an ID card through a reader. "Believe me, it's not easy to break into a jail that's on lockdown."

No wonder it had taken him so long to get back to my cell.

He flipped a switch. The outer door clicked open. He grabbed my arm and ushered me out.

"Thanks for the gun."

"It comes with a price."

"I'm a little short right now."

He hustled me down the hall, half crutch, half bulldozer. "You're going to tell me everything you know about this case, or so help me, Jack, I'll plant your ass in the middle of Civic Center Park with a sign on your back that says *I'm Jack Sabre, shoot me now.*"

"What happened to my twenty-four hours?"

"I changed my mind, partner."

That sent a jolt through my body that made my knee bark. "Partner?"

"If you want your badge back, we're going to do this bust together."

Fuck. The foot-dragger? My money had been on him being the bastard who'd doctored the ME's report and switched the DNA sample that exonerated Martin Vallinski as Maria's killer. He'd manipulated the system from the inside to throw off the investigation. His sister owned the burned-down donut shop headquarters for Davis's Denver Drug Cartel. I didn't trust him as far as I could spit. And now he was my partner?

I was screwed, glued, and tattooed.

Chapter Twenty-Three

DUSK.

The end of Mina's first day of captivity. I could only hope she was still alive, that Harman would want her as a means of getting to me. Problem was, I'd given him a good reason to kill her. I'd stuck my nose into their cocaine donut extravaganza and came up with shit in my nostrils and Detective Peterson on my back.

He swung his fancy Crown Vic into the Star Bar parking lot. Since Salvador was killed, Peterson had been promoted to supervisor. I knew this because an 870 Remington pump shotgun rode clamped in the dash bracket. Patrol officers and detectives carried non-lethal beanbag bangers with red stocks. Riding in the passenger seat next to the shotgun, I had plenty of leg room to extend my bad knee. And the windshield gave me a clear view of the pale stick furniture piled in the alley.

What the fuck had Porky done now?

Peterson shoved the shifter into park and killed the engine. "Every cop on the force will be looking for you, Jack."

"Yeah. They don't take kindly to jailbreaks. But don't forget, it was your idea."

"And now you're going to tell me who's behind all the killing."

I looked at him real hard while I mulled over how I was going to break the bad news to him. Real slow, like getting into a hot tub. "I don't trust you, Benny."

"That's your problem. Spill it."

"Let me tell you what I think."

"I don't give a fuck what you think."

"You swapped the DNA results and threw the investigation off track."

"I'm not playing tit for tat with you, Jack."

"Prove you didn't do it."

"I don't have to prove shit to you. The ME's report is legit."

"Then you won't have any problem rechecking the original sample. Right?"

"And if I do?"

"You'll find it was Vallinski's DNA under Maria's fingernails."

"And if I don't find his DNA?"

I inhaled and stared at the perfectly good furniture tossed in the alley. Reminded me of myself, a perfectly good cop kicked off the force. "I'll take your word for it." I wouldn't have said that if I wasn't positive I was right. Peterson had a long way to go before I trusted him on any level.

"All right. I'll check on the DNA sample. Now tell me who is trying to kill you."

"I can't. Not until tomorrow night."

"You lousy fuck." He yanked the radio mike off the dash clip. "I push this button and say I spotted the fugitive at the Star Bar—"

"All right." If he did that, this place would be swarming with cops. I had to stay out of jail long enough to nail Harman. The only way was to appease Peterson before he went all tattletale on me. "I can't tell you who they are because they've got Mina."

"Mina Finetree?"

"Tomorrow night they're supposed to let her go, after they settle up with some business deal. If I...if we interfere before then, she's dead, if they haven't killed her already."

"What makes you think they might have killed her?"

"They drove by the donut shop fire. They saw me. I shouldn't have been there."

"Goddammit, Jack."

"I was told to back off, and I didn't."

"Why didn't you say something?"

"Because they're mine."

"We're partners."

"Sorry, partner, this one's personal."

"And look what it's got you. Now Mina's life is on the line? For christsake. This is way over your head."

I'd heard that before. From Salvador. "I need another day, Benny. If I tell you who they are, you've got to let me handle this until then. Don't jump the gun on me."

He slammed the radio mike back into the holder. "You can't handle this on your own."

"I can and I will, but you've got to promise me—"

"You know the rules. I've got to report to the brass."

"And they'll send in SWAT all macho and

blasting away. Mina's as good as dead. What you don't know can't hurt her."

"Then I don't want to know. If she's dead, if she gets killed, it's gonna be on you, Jack. Now get out of my car."

"So you'll check on the DNA?"

"I'll see what I can find. Meanwhile, stay out of trouble."

I wanted to call him an asshole, but he did save my life. "Thanks." I got out, slammed the door, and stagger-stepped back on my bad leg.

He fired up the engine and slammed reverse, squealing tires then fishtailed onto Larimer and roared away. Fuckin' hot-head. Maybe he wasn't much different than me after all.

Stepping into the Star was like fast forwarding into the future. My eyes wanted to vomit. Those leather booths Porky had talked about lined the left side of the narrow room. Flat screens on the walls broadcasted ball games and the evening news. Center floor, new tables and chairs made of polished dark wood were lined in two neat rows, complete with lighted candles flickering inside little round bowls.

How dainty.

Heart panging, I walked past a new pool table, not a scratch on it, a dart board on the wall behind it, all lit up, and a jukebox with flashing lights. The real shocker was some contraption with a high-back seat, steering wheel, and video screen. Disney World it wasn't, but it wasn't the Star, either.

My gaze swiveled to the bar. A couple guys sat at one end, yuppies, one wearing thick glasses, the other a sweater vest his mother probably knitted for him. They sipped on cocktail straws in shallow glasses. Their barstools were new, tall bamboo jobs with padded seats, but the bar was the same chewed two-by-four rim and scarred top. Thank God.

I hobble-hopped to my usual spot, my hallowed ground, and touched Maria's carved name with a shaky fingertip. "Hello," I whispered and sat down. Home at last.

"One drink is all you get, mister," a woman's voice said.

I looked up, totally amazed that I wasn't looking at Porky but some broad with big tits penned up in a low-cut halter. A jewel the size of the Hope Diamond sparkled in her navel. Shirley

Terry Wright

Temple curls framed her soft face, but tight lips told me she was not America's sweetheart.

"One drink is all?"

"Then you hit the road. We don't want your kind in here."

"My...my kind?"

"Look at yourself."

I glanced down at my clothes, what was left of the chauffeur's uniform, torn shirt, sooty and blood splotched, and wrinkled like I'd slept in it. Just to be thorough, I sniffed my armpit. Smelled like smoke and sweat. I peered over her shoulder to the circle-star engraved mirror, didn't recognize the bum looking back at me. "Only one?"

"One." She seemed pretty sure of herself. "What'll it be?"

Still, that was one drink more than Porky would approve. "Make it a double shot of Old Crow. Straight up."

She cocked a sleek brow at me. "That's two drinks. You're a little pushy, don't you think?"

"You don't know the half of it."

She sighed, set a spotless glass in front of me, and poured whiskey from the bottle through a chrome spout.

What was this fucking world coming to?

"That'll be nine bucks."

"Nine bucks?" I shouted.

That earned me derisive glances from the yuppies sitting down the bar from me. I was about to tell them to mind their own fucking business when the barmaid cut me short. "Cash."

"Put it on my tab."

"You don't have a tab."

"Then start me a new one."

"Do I have to call a cop?"

"I am a cop." I lied. *Was a cop.*

She staggered back, sputtering like she was about to bust out in laughter.

Thinking fast, I downed the drink, fire and fumes old friends of mine. "Ask Porky. He'll spot me the cash."

"He's out shopping."

I wheezed. "Hasn't he spent enough on this joint for one day?"

"They've been working non-stop to renovate this old dive bar. Now he's only got one thing left to do. Replace this old bartop."

Shock slugged me like a fist to my temple. I slapped my hand over Maria's name, protectively.

"He can't."

She leaned forward. "What's under there?"

"Under where?"

"Your hand. What are you hiding?"

I wasn't hiding anything, I was protecting my sanctuary. It was all I had left of Maria. My eyes watered.

Bar girl looked at me with squinty eyes. "Don't tell me you're going to cry."

"Whiskey tears." I lied again.

"Show me what you've got there."

Hell, she'd find out anyway, next time she ragged down the bar. I slid my hand off Maria's name. "My dead wife. He can't replace this bar. It's my hallowed ground."

She straightened. "I see."

"What am I going to do now?" Fresh tears stung my eyes, real tears that I wouldn't blame on the whiskey. "Where will she end up? In the dump? Burned like scrap wood? No. He can't do this to her."

"How long has she been gone?"

"Six months."

"You poor man."

I ogle-eyed the Old Crow.

She looked at the bottle then set it in front of me, next to the empty glass. "Don't make me regret this."

My angel. Blinking away tears, I pulled out the chrome spout and poured right from the naked bottle neck. Just like old times. I lifted the glass, gentle as any flower. "Thanks."

She patted the bartop, said, "Good luck," and turned away.

Down the hatch Old Crow went, its hot and merciless wings fluttering with fury. My salvation. The cops may have been looking for me, APB and all, and Johnny Harman's goons with their guns and body armor wanted me dead, but right now I didn't give a flying fuck. And Benny Peterson could kiss my ass too. I was headed to whiskey heaven.

I poured another glass of sunshine, drank it down, and easily slipped into whiskey's warm embrace. One more. Two more. The Star began to feel soothing as sleep. I caressed Maria's name. "I miss you," I whispered and refilled the glass. "But we have to talk."

The next shot went down smoother than the last. I set the bottle and glass aside then assumed the position, forehead down on my forearms encircling her carved name. Anyone who walked in might think I was passed out on the bar.

"Do you remember Mina Finetree?" I whispered. "Yes...your dad's receptionist. I got her in a lot of trouble...she might be dead, but if not...you have to understand, she needs me now."

The skin on my shoulder tingled. Maria's soft touch. She always stood beside me at times like this, when I was snockered and missing her. Now I had to tell her these heart-to-hearts were going to end.

"Porky is going to throw you away."

I sniffed. Her carved name deformed in my alcohol bleary eyes.

"Everything is changing so fast...no, Mina is not my lover...yes, I do...of course I want to...not that...I want to save her...kiss her?...well, that too...please don't be mad, but I've got to move on with my life..."

"How could you, Jack?"

"I'm not leaving you...I know you're hurt...but no, Maria, it's got nothing to do with your glass eye..."

"Jack."

"It's not what you think...yes, she's beautiful—"

"Are you out of your mind, Jack?"

"No...I'm not...Maria... Do I look crazy?"

"You're drunk."

"Huh? That's nothing new...I'm always drunk when I talk to you. What are you bitching for now?

"Jack. Wake up."

The tingling in my shoulder changed to violent shaking. Whiskey's numb arms dropped me back to reality. I popped my head up, blinked, "What?" then swiveled the barstool around and came face to face with Helen, all curvy in a tight blouse and skirt. I was busted. "What are you doing here?"

"Jack, you're talking to yourself."

"I was sayin' goodbye to Maria."

"What for?"

"Look around. Porky is fucking up my Star."

She sat next to me. "I think the place looks great."

"You don't understand. He's going to tear out the whole fuckin' bar, along with her name.

Her shrine. Her memory."

Helen glanced down at Maria's name. "Don't be stupid, Jack. She's not linked to this bar. You are." Then she had the nerve to wave the new bartender over. "Coffee, please, two cups."

"Hey, I'm not done drinking."

"We brought you a present. You want to see it?"

"A present? What for?"

She stood and grabbed my arm. "On your feet, sailor."

I got my ass out of the yuppie-butt barstool. "Where are we goin'?"

"Outside."

I managed to get my leg to work, but my brain wanted to trip me up, dizzy and all. She helped me to the door and pushed through. Under the neon Star Bar sign leaned a black Harley Heritage. It had all the tits and tassels: twin chrome pipes, mini Ape handle bars, cruise control throttle lock, Easy Rider foot pegs. Nice bike.

Helen led me to the bike and smiled. "What do you think?"

Confusion hit me like a whiskey bottle over

the head. Cool bike. Whose bike? "What am I supposed to think?"

"Look in the rearview mirror."

Wobbly as a sick whore, I leaned to the handlebar rearview and saw the same bum I'd seen in the circle-star mirror inside. "So what? I need a shave."

"Take a good look," she said, "at the owner of this motorcycle."

This wasn't my bike. I wasn't drunk enough to forget buying a twenty-five thousand dollar Harley...then it hit me. The present? A Harley? "Are you out of your ever-lovin' — ?"

A voice behind me said, "You don't need to thank me, Jack."

I turned. Mrs. Vallinski. My jaw could've been a boat anchor on the Bismarck.

Danny stood beside her, helmet tucked under his left arm, riding gloves choked in his fist. "She runs sweet, Jacko."

This couldn't be the same Danny, sober enough to ride. I'd never seen him sober enough to walk.

He handed me the key fob that dangled from a winged Harley keychain. "Don't wreck this one."

I stared at the key in my upturned palm. Breathing no longer seemed possible. Swallowing too. I looked up at Mrs. Vallinski. "You didn't have to—"

"It's the least I could do, saving my life like you did. Now let's get some coffee in you. We've still got to find Mina."

Helen turned me toward the Star. "I'm disappointed in you, Jack. Drinking again."

"Join the club." I cranked my head around to look back at the bike. It was a virgin, all clean and pretty, with no memory of Maria sitting on the chrome studded leather seat or her arms wrapped around me as we cruised the mountain curves. Our ride was over. Now it wasn't hard to picture Mina seated there, riding with me into a new life with endless possibilities.

But first I had to save her.

Chapter Twenty-Four

I NEVER THOUGHT I'd see the time when Danny and I sat at the Star and drank coffee together. We'd settled around one of Porky's fancy new tables. His new clientele filtered in, downtown business types bent on cheering at those stupid flat screens. Even the two yuppies at the end of the bar joined in the brouhaha.

Before long I was a wide-awake drunk. I'd set the Harley key fob in front of me as motivation to continue downing caffeine. Mrs. Vallinski returned from Biker Jim's across the street and brought back bacon-wrapped hotdogs for our dinner. If Harman didn't kill me, I'd die of cardiac arrest.

After I ate, we watched the ten o'clock news and video of the donut shop fire. One dead. Smoke inhalation. I guessed she knew too much and had to die. Then the news lady talked about the shooting at city jail. Several wounded. One dead shooter. *Thanks to me.* I expected to see my picture splashed all over the screen. *Escapee wanted. Manhunt under way.* But nothing was said, which meant the department wanted to keep my jailbreak hushed up and avoid a black eye over bad publicity.

Helen set down her empty coffee cup. "Feeling any better now, Jack?"

"A little." My slide back to the dark side hadn't lasted long.

"Sober enough to drive?"

"I'm waiting for Peterson." As much as I wanted to give that new bike a spin, I had to be here when he got back.

"We can't wait all night."

"It's important."

Yuppies cheered at the TVs. I wished they'd quit making this a happy bar, had half a notion to pull the Glock from my waistband and shoot holes in the flat screens.

"Where will we go?" Mrs. Vallinski asked her. "My place isn't safe. And the cops are bound to have Mina's house staked out, and Jack's, too.

We should stay here. Lay low."

"Porky won't mind," I added.

"I'm not sleeping in this bar," Helen said. "I was hoping to get Jack into a shower and clean clothes. We can do that at my house."

The mayor's mansion. "Daddy's not going to be pleased with you bringing home a drunken bum."

"He's throwing some shindig for his political buddies tonight. He won't even notice you."

"I never go unnoticed, or haven't you noticed."

She shrugged.

I swigged cold coffee. "I'm not leaving. Once Peterson finds out I'm right about the DNA, I'll tell him that Harman and Davis are behind the murders. DPD will take over."

"You can't involve the police," Helen said. "Not until we get Mina back."

"I made a deal with him in exchange for a get out of jail card."

"You made a deal with Harman to lay off until tomorrow night. You pick and choose who you're going to be honest with?"

"Cops lie," I said. "It's how we get to the truth."

"Lotta good it does you," Danny put in. "Now Harman's out to kill you."

"If I renege on Peterson, he locks me up again, and Harman gets another crack at me. I mean the guy has enough balls to attack the city jail. I'll have to stay off Peterson's leash."

Helen tisked. "Just let him handle it, Jack."

"No way. Harman burned down his headquarters, for Christ sake. Why would he do that?"

"Destroy evidence," Helen said. "Why else?"

"So he knew I'd go there..." I looked at Danny Boy. "You're the one who told me it was his headquarters."

"Hey! Don't look at me."

Mrs. Vallinski tapped my arm. "You're smart, Jack, and he knows it."

"He's always one jump ahead of me. That must make him smarter."

"So jump backwards," Helen said. "What's the last thing he expects you to do?"

"How should I know?"

Black Jack

"Think about it. What's the last thing you want to do?"

That was easy. "Trust Harman to release Mina on his word alone."

"So do that."

"But I don't trust him." Besides, I wanted to wreck the business deal he had going down tomorrow night. "You guys go ahead. I'll catch up with you in the morning."

Helen stood. "No more drinking, or I'll take the Harley key with me."

"Got it."

Mrs. Vallinski stood, too. "Goodnight, Jack. Get some rest."

I couldn't rest until Mina was safe.

They walked out together.

"Think I'll get a beer." Danny slinked to the bar.

I wadded up hotdog wrappers. Two couples left the booth, staggered out, high-class drunks, I guessed. The place was thinning out. Even the two yuppies at the bar got up. One tossed change down for a tip. Peterson better get here pretty damn quick or I'd be sitting here all by myself. Sober.

I reached under the table and rubbed my sore knee with both hands.

The yuppies brushed by me. I looked away, didn't want to show them the disdain on my face. They swiveled around, pulled guns, and pointed cannon-sized barrels at me. "Go easy, Jack," the yuppie wearing glasses said.

Fear and surprise both had a stranglehold on my throat. I could barely croak out, "You've gotta be shittin' me."

"The Boss wants to see you." That came from his sweater-vested buddy. "So be cool."

Four Eyes flicked his gun at Danny by the bar. "Go out the back door." Then at the bartender. "You too, bitch." And the handful of patrons. "All of you. Move it. Down the alley and don't look back."

A scuffle and they were gone. I hoped one of them had a cell phone and the gumption to call 911.

My hands were still on my bad knee. I started moving them toward my waistband, real slow. "Who's your boss?"

"On your feet, Sabre."

"Hey! I've got a bum knee here."

Both barrels were trained on me again. If these clowns had orders to kill me, I'd have been dead already.

"Quit stalling."

"Give us your gun."

"I don't have a gun." I straightened just enough to free the Glock with my right hand, concealed by the table, and like any good magician, I misdirected their attention to my left hand by draping my left arm across the chair-back next to me, real casual. "Can we talk about this like gentlemen?"

"We ain't no gentlemen," Sweater Boy said and honked at his own joke.

I angled the gun up at Four Eyes, still under the table out of their line of sight. If these guys didn't back off, I'd have to blow a hole through Porky's new furniture. "Who are you working for?"

"We're not that stupid to tell you."

"Then I'm not stupid enough to go with you."

The yuppie goons glanced at each other.

I detected their jitters. "Tell me where we're going, I'll go with you. Your boss gets what he wants. You get a job-well-done pat on the back, and I know where I'm going. Simple as that. We all win."

"And if not?" Four Eyes asked.

"I kill you both."

That got a laugh out of them. Not funny. I pulled the trigger. The bang sounded like a howitzer blast. Wood splinters flew through the air. The bullet thunked into Four Eyes' chest. He fired his gun wildly on his way to the floor.

I'd already ducked under the table and shot a leg out from under Sweater Boy, even as his bullets thwacked into my chairback. He dropped his gun and started screaming, hopped around like a one-legged duck then flopped on his back, hugging his leg. I slammed my right knee across his throat, pinned him down, and pressed my gun barrel to his forehead. "Where is she?"

"The boss?" he rasped.

Why did he equate *she* with *boss*? "Mina Finetree, you bozo."

"I'm just the messenger, damn it." His words came out Donald Duckish.

I hit him with the gun butt, smack in the left temple. "Where is she?"

"All right. The mayor's mansion. She's at the mayor's mansion."

"What the fuck?" Helen and Mrs. Vallinski were headed there right now. A trap?

"I need a doctor."

A siren screamed up outside. 911 to the rescue. I got up off Sweater Boy. "Hang tight. We'll get you to the hospital."

He pulled a derringer from his sock. I barely caught the motion, shot him between the eyes, and dodged the spray of blood. "Cancel that."

The front door slammed open. Peterson stalked in, gun fanning the air. "You all right, Jack?"

"Do I look all right?"

He paced past me sweeping his gun like a radar probe under the tables, the booths, behind the bar. "Who the hell are those guys?"

"Old friends of mine. What do you think?"

I leaned over Four Eyes, checked for a pulse, but judging from the blood pool around him, he'd bled out fast.

Peterson kicked open the door to the john. "Clear!"

I gathered up the bad guys' guns, patted their pants, came up with a couple clips, and took inventory. I needed more ammo than this to lay siege on the mayor's mansion.

Peterson joined me. "You were right, Jack. Vallinski's DNA was under Maria's fingernails. Someone doctored the ME's report."

"I told you so." I shoved the clips in my pockets. "Someone with a lot of clout inside Denver PD."

"It wasn't me."

"It's not the first time I've been wrong about this case."

"I discovered something else."

"Good for you." I tucked the three guns behind my waistband. Made breathing a little difficult.

"It's disturbing, Jack."

"Then disturb me."

"The original coroner's report said Maria's glass eye was gone."

I stopped breathing. "Gone?" Harman's signature kill: plucking out an eyeball. The sick fuck. He was with Vallinski when he killed Maria. I imagined Harman stepping up to her dead body and popping out her glass eye...for a souvenir. If I could kill him twice, I would, once for Maria, once for her father, oh, and once more for the donut shop girl.

"Jack, we'll find it."

"Don't bother. I know who has it."

"Who?"

Peterson had come through on his part of the deal. Now it was my turn, but I wasn't ready to give up everything. I'd have one chance to set things straight, get even, and avenge Maria so we could both rest in peace. Stalling, I inspected the bullet hole I'd punched through Porky's new table. It was made of pressed wood, fake fine furniture. Made in China. Good chance I'd be dead right now if not for Porky's frugality.

"You better not jerk me around, Jack. Give me a name."

"Davis," I said.

"Ray Davis? The mayoral candidate?"

"None other." Now for the magician's misdirect. I kicked Sweater Man's corpse. "He told me Davis and his drug gang are holed up at the Mission on Park Avenue." I was getting good at this lying gig. "Right around the corner from here."

"Davis runs a drug gang?" Peterson
holstered his gun. "Do you know how ridiculous
that sounds?"

"It gets worse. His cocaine is being shipped
in donut boxes." No lie. "A big order is going out
tomorrow night. I was hoping to bust Davis and
his drug operation, both at the same time. Now
he's all yours."

"Do you have proof Davis killed Captain
Salvador?"

"He told me he did it." I lied. Harman did
it. "That's good enough proof for me. So go get
him."

"Thanks, Jack. I'll call this in." He glanced
at the dead guys. "And I'll pull surveillance off
your apartment. Go home and clean up, get some
rest. Denver PD will handle Davis from here."

"And my badge?"

"I'll talk to the DA in the morning. It'll take
some time to clear this mess up."

"Thanks, Benny."

"That's what partners are for, right?"

What a sap.

I limped out of the bar, Harley keychain in

hand, fully intent on leaving until I spotted Peterson's Crown Vic idling at the curb, grill lights flashing, driver door cocked open. He'd definitely been in a hurry when he'd bailed out. The shotgun poised upright against the dash grabbed my attention. More firepower. I leaned in and slapped the hidden release lever on the bracket. The shotgun fell into my hand, Peterson's real-deal Remington pump. Loaded.

He would be pissed at me for borrowing it, but by then this would all be over.

Terry Wright

Chapter Twenty-Five

SIRENS SHRIEKED in the distance. Peterson's backup was on the way. All I needed was some gung ho rookie to hold me for questioning.

I rushed to my new Harley, and pivoting on my bad leg, I threw my good leg over the seat. The guns behind my waistband poked my kidneys. I shoved the shotgun between my right thigh and the seat and stabbed the key fob into my pocket. As much as it killed my left knee, I cranked the bike upright off the kickstand and anticipated the rush of wind in my hair. What I got was an unexpected jerk on the suspension.

Danny had jumped on behind me. "Go, Jacko! Go."

"What the hell? Get off—"

Tires squealing, a Black Lincoln careened

around the corner onto Larimer Street. The dead yuppies must've had backup in case they didn't make it out of the Star Bar alive.

"Son of a bitch." I twisted the ignition and punched the start button. The big V-Twin fired first try. Instead of thunder, I heard a muffled rumble.

Potata-potata-potata.

The Lincoln's headlights barreled toward me. Traffic on Larimer swerved and honked.

I forced my screaming left knee to bend enough to toe the shifter into gear. One down. Four up. I twisted the throttle and popped the clutch. Tires hit the blacktop.

The goons in the Lincoln opened fire.

Cars careened out of the way, crashed into each other, slammed poles and parking meters.

I zigged and zagged through traffic and blew the first stop light. If I wasn't still a little drunk, I'd have scared the hell out of myself.

Danny hung on to me like a biker bitch.

In my left rearview mirror, the Lincoln leaned on its springs as it swerved up behind us. Muzzles flashed from the passenger side. Sonic cracks zinged past my head. The mirror shattered.

My Harley could outdistance the car but not the bullets. I had to do something to make them back off. Maybe Danny could be of some use. "Can you shoot?" I shouted back at him?

"Not since Iraq. I'd forget—"

"Good enough." I worked a gun out from my waistband. The Luger that once belonged to Sweater Man came out. "Take this and unload the clip on those bastards."

Danny took the gun like it might sting him. "I don't know."

A bullet zinged by my head. "Just do it or we're both dead."

He twisted around and fired. In my right rearview, the Lincoln nosed down under full braking power. Smoke swirled from the tires.

I guessed the bad guys didn't want to get their paint job scratched. Well, I had news for them. They weren't getting off that easy.

"Hang on."

Danny's arms looped around my chest. I felt the heat of the gun barrel under my chin and hoped the clip was empty. Now to take the offensive. I squeezed the shotgun to the seat with my thigh and stomped on the rear brake pedal.

Nothing like new disc brakes to lock up a tire. I leaned hard left so the bike skidded around to stop facing the wrong way in traffic, which had come to a standstill, headlights silhouetting the black Lincoln down the block.

I gunned the engine. A lawnmower could have sounded more threatening.

Tires smoking, the Lincoln surged forward.

I revved the V-Twin to redline and popped the clutch. The Harley nearly jumped out from under me. Rear tire churning, I punched through the gears then locked the throttle thumb wheel.

"Fuck!" Danny yelled and shoved his face into my back.

Bearing down on the speeding Lincoln, I let go of the handle bars, yanked the shotgun up, pumped the first of five shells into the chamber, shouldered the gun butt, and fired.

Boom!

A buckshot pattern blossomed on the Lincoln's windshield.

Annie Oakley, eat your heart out.

I pumped again. Fired.

Steam geysered from the Lincoln's grill. Muzzle flashes blazed from the passenger window.

A taxi came out of nowhere, got in the way, skidded out of control, and plowed into a parked pickup.

I leaned right, leaned left, pumped and fired again. Buckshot tore the hand off the goon shooting from the passenger side. Gun, flesh, and bone bounced on the asphalt.

I pumped. Fired.

The right front tire shredded. Sparks flew. The car swerved right, crossed in front of me, and gave me a clear shot at the driver's window, not two car-lengths away. Harman wasn't driving. Just another one of his hired thugs.

I pumped.

I fired.

Glass exploded, along with the driver's skull. The Lincoln plowed over the sidewalk, caught righteous air, dive-bombed a row of newspaper boxes, and slammed into the Volunteers of America Building.

"All right!" Danny shouted.

I released the throttle lock and braked hard. Several blocks down Larimer Street, flashing emergency lights converged on the Star Bar. Good

money said there'd be heavy police activity
around the *Jesus Saves* mission, as well. I whipped
a u-ee and throttled past the wreck. Within
minutes, this area would be a roped-off crime
scene.

DPD would have their hands full tonight.

And so would I.

***

I coasted the Harley into my parking
garage, not a police car anywhere in sight.
Peterson had called off his dogs. The mayor was
having a party tonight. Danny and I were going to
crash it. We'd discussed the details on the ride to
my place, decided we couldn't go in looking like
Larimer Street bums.

Danny hopped off the bike and handed me
the Lugar. "I don't know how you do it, Jacko,
killing all those guys. Doesn't it bother you?"

"Not today." I stuffed in a fresh clip I'd
taken off Sweater Boy. "They started this war."
The gun went back in my waistband. "Now I'm
going to finish it." I got off the bike. "Tomorrow
it'll bother me."

Limping, I led the way to my apartment,

wishing Danny hadn't made me think about how I felt about killing scumbags. They each had some stake in Davis's drug business, enough so that they'd kill anyone who got in their way. Lately, that had been me, so I was merely executing my right to protect myself. That didn't make pulling the trigger any easier, but I wouldn't argue with necessity. Question was, if shit hit the fan, could Danny pull the trigger? I hoped I wouldn't have to find out.

Inside, I showered while Danny thumbed through my girly magazine collection. Shaving was no easy task with all the welts and cuts I had to maneuver the blade around. I wished Mina was here to nurse me. I'd get her back tonight if Harman didn't kill me first.

While Danny cleaned up, I laid out a suit for him, an old one that had shrunk in my closet over the years. I chose a much newer suit, a tuxedo I'd worn when I married Maria. Memories banged at my mental back door, but I refused to answer, refused to let them in, refused to allow my focus to be distracted from saving Mina. I had to look my best. The tux was a necessity. The memories were not.

I adjusted the cummerbund, a perfect place to hide my gun. The bow tie was a clip-on job.

Danny walked in, hair slicked back, towel around his waist. "Why do I feel like I just took my last shower?"

"Follow my lead, you'll be okay." I tossed him a pair of clean skivvies.

He dropped the towel and stepped into them. "But I'm the one whose ass will be on the line."

"What's so hard about creating a disturbance? Just be yourself."

"It's easier when I'm drunk."

"No drinking." Imagine me giving that advice. I leveled my bow tie in the mirror. "And don't do anything until I find Mina."

He stepped into a pair of slacks, a bit baggy for his skinny frame, but they'd have to do. As he shrugged into one of my white shirts he asked a legitimate question. "Do you think Mayor Hodges is in bed with Davis?"

"I doubt it. They're running opposed in the election."

"But if they are, where does that leave Helen?"

"Shut up and get dressed." I didn't want to think that Helen had been screwing with me all this time. As far as I knew, she and Mrs. V. had walked into a trap. They were probably tied up already, in chairs. Harman had a fetish for tying up women and plucking out their eyeballs.

Pissed me off just thinking about it.

***

The mayor's mansion took up eight lots in the Hilltop section of Denver. Built by cable TV mogul Bill Daniels, the house was donated to the city to be used for the official mayor's residence and nonprofit fundraising events. High stockade fences and laser security surrounded the opulent estate.

I coasted the Harley up to the mansion's wide driveway, Surprised to see the gate open for the festivity's guests. A couple cars idled ahead of me. An attendant waved us in. Security guards would surely give us the once-over inside, Denver cops working off duty, most likely. I carried one gun. Danny, straddling the seat behind me, had two, one for making noise, one for back up. I hoped the guards didn't have metal detectors.

"You ready?" I asked Danny.

"I need a drink."

"Toughen up, my man, toughen up." I knew I had to. Who wouldn't rather be drinking than crashing the mayor's party?

I aimed the bike down the driveway that ran between manicured pines and soft ground lighting. Expensive cars were neatly parked at angles to the house, probably a valet service's doing, but I found enough space by the *Cableland* sign to park the Harley myself.

It wasn't until we reached the front steps that anyone ran interference. Some broad-shouldered man in a three piece suit stopped us. "Invitations, gentlemen." He held his hand out, palm up.

I could smell a goon a mile away. This one stunk like Pepe LePew. What was he doing here? Where were the Denver cops who normally guarded the mayor? Where were the uniformed security guards for Cableland? Davis and his band of drug dealers were here, all right, and I had a bad feeling they'd hijacked this party, taken hostages inside.

"Well?" the goon said, rubbing his

fingertips together impatiently.

I glanced up at the security camera over the door and hoped someone was watching me bluff my way in. "Special envoy to the mayor," I said. "We don't need no stinking invitations." I stepped up the step.

The goon put his fat hand against my tux. "You take another step, I'll break your fucking leg."

Damn! Now I'd have to pull out my gun and shoot the bastard, which would throw off my plan to rescue Mina by a light year.

Another goon rushed up and stood next to his buddy. "Problem here?"

I looked at Danny. "You got a problem?"

He shrugged.

Guess I'd have to kill them both. Danny would probably wonder if that would bother me to waste these two bastards. It had better not bother me. One second's hesitation could cost me my life. Danny should've kept his mouth shut about my feelings. I started to reach for the gun under my cummerbund when a woman's voice came from behind the wall of thugs. "It's okay, boys. They're with me."

They stepped apart, revealing Helen. She wore a sleek red gown that hugged her body from tits to ankles. Silver high heels matched the jeweled band around her neck. Good thing I hadn't yet grabbed my gun, I'd have shot myself in the foot.

"Come in, please," she said.

I wedged between the goons. Danny trailed me. I trailed Helen. She pushed open the front doors. Strains of classical music drifted out. We stepped inside together.

The foyer overlooked an immense front room with floor-to-ceiling windows and soft lighting recessed behind geometric shapes. Richly dressed men and women milled about, conversing softly. Danny and I would fit right in with this bunch.

I spotted Mrs. Vallinski, all dolled up in a frilly white dress, setting pretty on a cushy couch. A ritzy looking gentleman sat with her. She had his full attention.

Helen leaned against the brass railing. I nodded to Danny, his signal to mingle, and then stood next to Helen.

Danny charged down the curved staircase

and headed to the bar. Shit! I'd told him no drinking.

Helen glanced at me, a party glint in her eye. "You clean up real nice, Jack. Guess you found a shower."

"My place." I sidled up closer to her, my eyes scanning the crowd for Davis and Harman and the mayor. Not present.

"Then what are you doing here?"

I leaned to her ear and whispered, "Where is your father?"

"Why are you whispering?"

"So nobody will hear me, what do you think? Where is he?"

She glanced down at the party-goers. "In his study, meeting with his election team. What's going on?"

I followed her gaze. Danny held a drink, a double shot of booze from the depth and color of the liquid in the glass. The son of bitch, he'd better not blow his assignment.

Helen slipped an arm around me. "What is it? You tensed up."

I pulled her close to watch her eyes. "Mina is here."

She didn't even blink. Shock shrank her pupils. Then: "That's crazy. Who told you that?"

"Some guy at the Star who tried to kill me. Didn't work out for him, though."

"You killed him?"

"Two of them. Davis's goons. Like the guys out front."

"Jack, you've got to stop killing people."

"I'm just getting started. Where is the regular security detail?"

"My father gave them the night off when those guys outside showed up, all of a sudden, too. I thought that was strange."

"It's a good bet Harman and Davis are here someplace. Where would they be holed up?"

Her eyes fluttered over my face like they were trying to find a place to land. "There're over nineteen-thousand square feet in this house. It's easy to host three events simultaneously without any of them knowing about the others..."

"Where could we start looking?"

"Video surveillance." She inhaled. "But the regular staff is gone. We'll need my dad's help to get into the control room."

"I don't want him to know we're here."

"Why not? He's got the access code. He can help us find Mina."

"Harman sent his goons to kill me, Helen. I can't take the chance that your father and Davis are working together."

She turned her back to me, crossed her arms. "It's not possible."

Glancing around, I could have believed her. Nothing seemed amiss, no hint the party was under siege. Sweater Man could have lied about Mina being here. But why would he? And the goons outside convinced me something underhanded was going down. I'd have to trust that Helen was right about her father. "All right. Let's ask him for his help."

Helen faced me. Smiled. "You'll see." She lifted her gown enough to bounce down the steps.

I followed her, not so bouncily, nursing my bad leg.

Danny raised his glass to me, almost empty. I wanted to snatch it from his hand and shove it up his ass. Instead, I sneered at him like a disapproving mother.

He smiled like he'd pulled one over on me.

We passed by a pair of elephant statues,

life-sized mother and baby under the glow of warm spotlights, and then I hobbled down a wide stairway to another huge gathering room full of couches and tables. Helen's high-heels clacked on the hardwood floor, past more flat screens and a fireplace.

A doorway led to a business center, computers and monitors, phones and faxes. Plush furniture and fancy desks. *Cableland* logos adorned the walls. Security cameras hovered in every corner.

My neck began to itch. I didn't like moving this far away from Danny. If I got into a jam, I wouldn't be able to signal him to start a ruckus and divert attention away from me. I'd be on my own.

She spread open French doors. "Dad."

I held back a step. Men in suits stood around, drinks in hand. Their heads turned to Helen. No familiar faces.

"I need your help," she said, still plowing forward.

"I'm in the middle of a meeting here, Helen."

Instinct told me to hold back another beat.

"Everybody, my daughter, Helen."

The men nodded.

It seemed to me that no one in the room had a clue about Davis, Harman, and Mina. Helen had already made it to where her father stood by a towering bookshelf. She whispered in his ear. The small, balding man looked at me over the top of his glasses. I stepped into the study.

Click. Click.

I froze. Davis stood on my right. Harman on my left. Each held a gun at my ears. I swallowed a boulder and raised my hands like I was being robbed.

Two pricks frisked me, careful as petting a rattler, took my gun, and stepped back.

Harman said, "How good of you to join us, Jack."

I was fucked.

Chapter Twenty-Six

THE TOWERING BOOKCASE levered away from the wall, exposing a brightly lit hallway. Davis gun-muzzled me forward. I hobbled past Helen, who stood slack-jawed next to her father. The shock in her eyes was evidence enough that she hadn't intended to lead me into a trap. Her father looked equally bewildered. I shrugged at her, and as I stepped up to the wall opening, she shouted at her father, "What the fuck is going on?"

The two pricks who'd taken my gun grabbed her, started hauling her out, kicking and screaming. Her silver high heels flew off and clattered across the floor like tossed beer cans. I gritted my teeth. If I moved to help her, I'd get gunned down, for sure. The suited men standing around seemed frozen in disbelief. Mayor Hodges' feet must've grown roots. He did nothing to aid his daughter. Then I glimpsed a man holding a gun on him and understood why.

Harman grabbed my arm and muscled me into the hallway. A security camera overlooked the small area. "Smile for the camera," I told him.

"They're all shut off, smartass."

Davis followed, gun at my back. "Don't look so surprised, Jack. Cableland has a lot of secret passageways and tunnels."

"So do snake dens and termite piles."

That earned me a gut punch from Harman.

Buckled over, I fought for air. He opened a door and shoved me into a windowless room with soundproof padding on the walls. A harsh spotlight shined on a steel chair set in the center of the floor. And behind that, hanging barely in the shadows, a woman's curvaceous body.

"Mina."

A yellow ball-gag kept her from answering. Harman had strung her up to the ceiling by chrome chains around her wrists, stripped her down to her black panties and bra, and shackled her bare feet to the floor, spread-eagle.

Rage blew through my brain like a

firestorm, but I had to stay cool and fought the urge to sucker-punch Harman. Davis would plug me in the back, for sure. I'd be no good to Mina dead, so I winked at her, hoping to ease her wide-eyed fear.

Davis dumped me into the steel chair. The armrests and foot pads could have made it comfortable if not for the leather straps that Harman cinched around my wrists and ankles. My left knee felt like it was going to snap and break my leg in two.

"End of the line for you, Jack," he said with a throaty growl.

Davis holstered his gun inside his jacket, smug in his assurance that I was sufficiently restrained.

I had them right where I wanted them.

Mina wriggled in her chains. I didn't see any marks on her body, so it was safe to assume she hadn't been tortured. Not yet anyway. The perimeter of the room lay in shadow, but spines of light reflected off shiny parts of a tread mill and exercise bike. Cozy little workout room turned torture chamber.

I scowled up at Harman. All he needed was

a hood and an axe to fit the role of dungeon master. I couldn't help but feel this was familiar territory for him. "Did you tie up Maria like that?" I tipped my head to Mina.

He slipped into a pair of black gloves and wiggled his fingers, casual as a gentleman at the opera.

I knew a beating was in my immediate future but didn't care. "Got your rocks off I'll bet."

He made a fist and slugged me in the jaw. My teeth banged together so hard I thought they would shatter like cheap china.

Mina squealed and squirmed.

I spit blood on Harman's shoes.

That backed him up.

My tuxedo jacket had bunched up on my chest and drew tight across my shoulders. That in itself was torture, along with not knowing Helen's fate. And good old Danny, he was probably oblivious to the jam I was in, drinking bourbon and waiting for my signal to raise a ruckus. Fat lot of good that would do me now.

Davis waddled up. "Couldn't keep your nose out of our business for one more day, could you, Jack?"

"Fuck you."

Harman chuckled. "I told you he couldn't resist causing trouble." He reared back to slug me again.

Davis stopped him. "Why do you have to be such an asshole, Jack. Now we've got to kill you."

If I had a nickel for every time someone threatened my life, I'd be living on a beach in Fiji. "I know about your donut delivery," I sputtered, my lower lip swelling. "Tomorrow night, a whole truckload, I hear. You might have fooled the drunks you hired to do the grunt work, but you didn't fool me. You're just a low-life cocaine dealer. Probably use the profits to finance your campaign."

Davis turned to one of his three henchmen standing guard and waggled a finger at him. He stepped into a dark corner and returned with a donut box, wrapped and tied just like Danny had described. He handed it to Davis who plopped it in my lap.

My knee panged. The box must've weighed seventy pounds. Definitely too heavy for cocaine.

The goon produced a knife and stepped

toward me like I was a pig he was about to gut. I gritted my teeth at him. *Go ahead, cut me, you fucker.* Instead, he cut the strings and peeled back the wrapper. Through the cellophane display window, greenbacks stared out at me. Franklins.

"Four hundred grand," Davis said.

I looked up, trying to wrap my head around a hundred of these boxes Danny had helped load into a truck. "The donut business that good?"

"Counterfeits, smartass, not perfect but good enough. Forty million bucks."

"So the donut shop was a front for counterfeiting, not drugs...and Maria found out."

"She was going to the cops," Harman said, his hand stuffed in his jacket pocket. "Couldn't have that, now could we?" He pulled out a gloved fist and opened his palm. "This look familiar?"

Maria's glass eyeball stared at me blankly.

For one second I thought the earth had stopped rotating. The ground opened up and hell's fire leaped out and ignited the sky. "You lousy fucking son of a bitch." I jerked my body around in the chair, trying to tip it over, but it must've been bolted to the floor. "I'll kill you, motherfucker."

Harman laughed, grabbed the knife from the goon's hand, and pressed it against the side of my neck. I had to stop thrashing or get my jugular slashed. He held Maria's eye up to my face. "I did this to her, Jack."

"You?"

"When she was a kid, I cut out her eye."

I couldn't take my terrorized gaze off the black pupil, like it was staring at me, and I had to stare back.

He pressed the blade to my neck with more force. "I'd watch her in that park, swinging on that swing. Oh, I tried to be friendly, but the bitch wouldn't kiss me, so I taught her a lesson."

Now I understood how Harman knew which park Salvador and I were meeting in that night. "And you got away with it."

"She'd never seen me before, couldn't identify me, and she hadn't seen me since, until she popped in at the donut shop uninvited and stuck her nose in Lila's business." He closed his fist around Maria's glass eye and dumped it back into his pocket. "Now you're next, Jack. Problem solved."

Mina whimpered behind the ball-gag.

I had to get her out of here. "Okay." I clenched my fists. "You've got me. That's what you wanted. Let Mina go."

Davis leered at her. "The boss's new play-toy. Isn't she a beauty?"

I shot Harman a fuck-you look. "Don't you touch her."

"Me?" He laughed. "Wouldn't think of it."

"Then let her go."

"Not on your life, Jack."

These guys wouldn't listen to reason. Maybe a bluff would change their minds. "I've got undercover cops stationed at this party. You can't get away with this."

Harman harrumphed. "The police don't scare us."

"Of course not. You have someone on the inside."

"We did," Davis said. "Captain Salvador."

I swallowed. My brain started glitching out like a faulty florescent tube. It couldn't have been Salvador. He'd paid Vallinski for a hit on the man responsible for Maria's death. That was how I had it figured. So... "If Salvador was your inside man, why did he hire Vallinski to kill you?" I glared at Harman.

He moved the knife tip up under my ear. "You think you have it all figured out, huh?"

I grimaced at the sharp edge poking my skin.

"Well, you're wrong again." Davis laughed. "Salvador paid Vallinski to kill *you*, Jack."

Mina whimpered.

"Me?" I choked out. Harman should just run the knife through my throat and get me the hell out of this nightmare. The captain made the last call to Vallinski's cell phone to pay for *my* murder? "Why?" was all I could mutter.

"You wouldn't back off the case," Davis said. "You had to be eliminated."

"I was his son-in-law, goddammit. I was family. Why would he do that?"

Harman backed off with the knife. "He tried to talk sense into you, but you wouldn't listen. We couldn't have you butting into our business, so we threatened to blow the whistle on him for tampering with evidence."

The only tampering I knew about was the ME's report. If Salvador had doctored it to clear

Vallinski and throw off the investigation, his career would have been over, not to mention prison time. Last place a cop wanted to go was prison. That was motivation enough to hire someone to have me killed. Guilty as charged. "He chose his career over his family."

Harman stepped back. "But he wasn't man enough to kill you himself."

My palms started to sweat. I'd inadvertently killed my executioner. "So he hired Vallinski, and after I killed him, Salvador either had to kill me or join me."

"He switched teams," Davis said. "Signed up with the losers."

"I had to kill him, Jack." Harman cackled. "But I had fun doing it. Damn near got his eyeball, too, except you showed up."

If Harman had a shovel, he couldn't have dug his grave any deeper. "I'm going to kill you, Johnny Boy, and I'm going to have fun doing it."

He slugged me again. I saw stars, spit blood, said, "Fuck!"

The door opened, spilling light into the room. Along the far wall, donut boxes were stacked floor to ceiling. What did Davis and his gang plan to do with forty million dollars worth of phony money?

A woman's voice shouted, "Davis!"

I squinted against the glare of the doorway that silhouetted the woman storming in. *I'll be damned.* Lila Peterson. Her appearance didn't surprise me near as much as the gun she stood behind.

"What the fuck is going on in here?"

The goons stepped back as she stalked toward Davis, her white lacy evening gown a whisper, hair tied up and flowered in a million-dollar 'do. I hardly recognized her without her boobs flopped out. "You just had to show him the money, didn't you?"

"He's going to be dead anyway. Doesn't matter."

"I warned you about him." She kneed Davis in the groin.

He bent over, cupped his jewels, and gasped.

I gasped too. She was one mean bitch.

Mina struggled in her chains, eyes wide like she was more afraid now than before.

And fear clouded Harman's eyes.

Lila pointed her gun at him and gave it a twitch. "Put the money back where it belongs."

"Yes, ma'am." He lifted the box off my lap. The wrapper and string fluttered to the floor, just like my stomach.

Davis coughed. "I've got this handled, boss."

"Shit you do."

So there I had it. Lila Peterson was the matriarch in this den of weasels. The Boss. Salvador had swallowed the oldest bait in the business. Pussy. Hook, line, and sinker. He'd bought into her scheme for love or sex or money or power, who knew, but good old pussy got him killed more than anything.

She spun around, gun pointed at me. "Do I have to kill him myself?"

"Shoot him," Davis groaned out.

Harman said, "I'm done with him."

My throat felt like I'd swallowed soot. I would have cast my nay vote, but the barrel of that gun pointed at my face robbed me of the word.

Mina squealed behind her ball-gag.

Lila looked at her and smiled. "I've got

other plans for you, honey." She lowered the gun and paced the few steps to Mina. "You're much too pretty to kill right away."

Mina squirmed.

That earned her the gun barrel between her legs, up high against her sweet spot.

She stopped squirming, eyes ringed in white.

Lila moved in closer, went face-to-face with Mina, and then licked her ball-gag, slowly with a long, fat tongue. "But you'll thank me when I'm done with you."

My stomach turned with a sickening sense of dread. "Leave her alone."

Lila stiffened then spun on Harman. "Kill him."

He came back with the knife and a smile on his face. "First, I'm going to cut out his eye."

I gritted my teeth. Maria's pain would now be my pain.

"Not here, you idiot," Lila shouted. "We've got a party going on. Gut him somewhere else and dump his carcass in the Platte River."

Harman grinned. "You're gonna be fish chum, Jack." He unbuckled my arm straps. "But

I'll have both your eyes in a mason jar."

Lila held her gun on me, the dare in her eyes unmistakable. If she knew that I wasn't going peacefully, she'd shoot me now.

My hands came free. I rubbed my wrists.

Harman knelt, unbuckled my right ankle, started on the left. In one second, he'd find out he made a big mistake.

"Boss?" Danny's voice?

I cranked my head to the door. So did Harman.

Danny stood there, hands shoved in his baggy pants pockets, casual as could be. "You want me to load them donuts for you?"

"What are you doing here?" Lila shouted and swiveled her gun barrel at him.

"Just trying to help, Boss."

"Get him out of here," she ordered her goons.

The three of them moved toward Danny.

He shifted his hands in his baggy pockets. The material poked outward and exploded. Big and macho like John Wayne he wasn't, but by God he'd cut those thugs down as if they were struck by lightning.

The noise stopped Harman cold. I kicked him in the head with my right foot.

As he fell backward, I levered up from the chair and flung myself forward into Davis, grabbing for the gun under his jacket. He cranked his body around to protect the gun. I couldn't move my left foot. The sudden strain twisted my bad left knee. Pain chewed up my leg like a rabid alligator. I didn't have the leverage or the strength to wrench him back around; he was stout as an old Buick. Teeth gritted, I hung on to his jacket.

Danny had both guns out, muzzles blazing. The drunk was blasting every goon who moved.

Out the corner of my eye, I saw Lila swing her gun toward me. I had to let go of the struggling fat man and drop to the floor. My kneecap resounded a loud pop.

Lila's gun banged.

Danny went down. "I'm hit."

"Danny!"

He tossed me a gun. It flip-floated toward me through the air.

Davis drew his gun from under his jacket. Lila angled her aim down on me. Mina thrashed on her chains.

Danny's gun hit my open right palm...and stuck.

I swept the business end to Lila and squeezed off two shots. *Bang. Bang.* Blood blossomed between her breasts.

As her legs gave out underneath her, I pivoted my sights on Davis and pulled the trigger.

Bang. Click.

Empty.

The bullet that hit Davis didn't get a reaction from him any worse than a bee sting. He winced but didn't go down. The fat fuck's belly was bulletproof.

"Shit."

He loomed above me, gun aimed down at my head. "You lose, Jack."

Bang!

He staggered backward, dropped the gun, and plopped over like the sack of shit he was. Blood gushed from the back of his head.

My eyes went to Danny; he wasn't moving. He hadn't fired the shot that saved my ass. I looked up to the doorway.

Mrs. Vallinski stood there, her purse pinched under her left arm, her right arm still extended, holding her gun. The look on her face was K-9 fierce. "That one's for my boy."

My leg felt like I had barbed wire for bones, but I had to endure the pain and stretch to get hold of Davis's dropped gun. Harman had to be only one gunshot away from my heart, one knife blade away from my throat. I turreted the barrel across the floor: from Danny to Davis to Mina. No feet, no Harman. Where the fuck did he go?

Helen rushed in, running stocking-footed to Mina. "I'm so glad you're all right," she cried and pulled out the ball-gag.

Mina spit. "Jack," she gasped, "trapdoor." She tilted her head in the direction I should look. "Get him."

I jackknifed my body to reach the strap on my left ankle. My leg was twisted so badly, the strap around my ankle was too tight to unbuckle. I'd have to stand up and sit in the chair, but I didn't have the strength or the time. Harman was getting away.

By now, Mrs. Vallinski had come to my assistance.

"Shoot the strap," I shouted.

She handed me the gun. "I don't want to

hurt you, Jack."

I took aim—what more harm could a bullet wound do?—and fired. The strap snapped and walloped my ankle, but I was free of the chair. My kneecap was now a lump on the outside of my leg. Combat-crawling in the direction Mina had indicated, I found a seam in the floor, well camouflaged in the hardwood pattern. No handle.

I tried to pry the boards up with my fingernails. No luck. A knife gouge in the wood showed me how Harman had opened the trapdoor. Son of a bitch. I didn't have a knife. Not a screwdriver, not a lousy fucking crowbar. Davis had mentioned secret passages and tunnels. Harman was probably halfway to Kansas by now. "Damn!"

Danny moaned.

I crawled to him. He was gut-shot and holding a blood-soaked hand over the bullet hole. A painful way to die. "Danny."

He coughed. "Did you get her...the Boss?"

"I got her, buddy." I propped myself up on my elbows beside him. "We're going to get you some help. Just hang on."

"I saw her...at the party." Danny

swallowed. "I followed her. I found you."

"Damn good shooting for someone who'd been drinking."

"Iced tea." He hacked up blood, spit. "You told me no drinking...Mina...is she all right?"

I looked behind me. Helen and Mrs. Vallinski had undone her wrist chains. They were bent over working on her ankle bracelets. She was looking at me with her arms crossed over her bra.

"She's going to be okay." I looked back at Danny. His eyes stared blankly into nowhere. My vision blurred behind burning tears.

Sucks to be a friend of mine.

Chapter Twenty-Seven

"JACK." MINA KNELT next to me and put a comforting hand on my back. "Is he...?"

"Danny's dead," I told her.

"Are you all right?"

I tore my gaze from Danny's wide-open stare and looked at Mina. Her hair hung down over the side of her face. "Yeah." I blinked. "Nothing knee replacement surgery won't fix."

"Can I help you up?"

I inhaled. "No thanks. I'll stay here with Danny."

"Jack," Helen shouted. "Look out!"

Behind Mina, a not-dead-enough goon raised a wobbly gun. Danny's second gun lay out of my reach. I grabbed Mina and rolled her over the top of me to the floor. Looping my arms around her, I shielded her body with mine and buried my face into her warm neck. If I had to die now, this would be the way to go.

Gunfire rang out in double-tap bursts. I looked up.

Peterson rushed in and kicked the now-really-dead goon's gun across the floor. Uniformed officers filed in, weapons drawn, but there was no one left standing to shoot. Not even Harman. The chickenshit bastard got away.

Mina whispered in my ear. "Thanks, Jack."

I squeezed her in my arms. "My pleasure." And I meant it.

"Goddamnit, Jack," Peterson shouted. "You sent me on a wild goose chase. The Mission, hell. I should shoot you myself."

Leave it to Peterson to fuck up a tender moment.

I released Mina, rolled on my back, and looked up at him standing in his famous Superman stance. "I told you, Benny, this was personal."

"You lied to me." He holstered his gun. "We had a deal. You don't lie to your partner."

We weren't really partners, not officially, but I'd let him think we were. "How did you know I was here?"

He looked at me with hard eyes. "Mayor Hodges called 911. Said his daughter and some guy named Jack Sabre were in trouble at Cableland. Dispatch notified me. They always call me when your name comes up. It's like a fucking curse."

"Stop whining and look behind you." I poked my chin toward the white lacy heap lying face-down on the floor. "Explain that."

He turned around.

A uniformed officer knelt next to Lila and checked her neck for a pulse. He looked up at Peterson. "She's dead."

"Roll her over, let's see who she is."

The officer said, "I don't know, detective. Shouldn't we wait for the M.E. before we move anything?"

I didn't have all night to play *What's My Line*. "Let me introduce you to the Boss, Benny."

"Vallinski's boss?"

"And Harman's and Davis's, everybody's boss. She was behind the killings. Maria, Salvador, the donut shop girl, and even Danny Boy here."

"Who is she?"

"Your sister."

His back stiffened as if I'd knifed him between the shoulder blades. "Lila?" He dropped to his knees and rolled her over himself. "Lila! What the fuck?" His eyes went to the blood stain on her dress. "Two shots. Dead center chest." Then he looked at me. "You shot my sister?"

"Sorry, Benny, but shit happens. It was self defense."

I watched Peterson choke back tears for his dead sister. He wouldn't show his emotions in public. Cops were tougher than real human beings, but he'd cry like a baby when no one was looking.

He stood. "Secure this crime scene," he told a uniformed officer.

Mrs. Vallinski rushed up to Mina. "I think these are yours." In one hand, she held out a white halter top and a pair of yellow shorts. In the other, a pair of Nikes.

"My clothes," she said as Helen gave her a helping hand off the floor. "Thanks."

As Mina got dressed, I levered my aching body up to a sitting position and scooted toward Danny's backup gun, hoping it wasn't empty.

Now that it was within reach, I asked Benny the forty-million-dollar question: "So you didn't know your sister was the mastermind of a counterfeiting ring that reached all the way to the mayor's office?"

He scowled at me as if I'd just poked him with a sharp stick. The air in the room seemed to freeze.

I moved my hand closer to Danny's gun.

Uniformed officers watched, their eyes darting between me and Peterson, as if waiting for one of us to make a wrong move. None of them wanted to tangle with me, and I was sure they'd take Peterson's side because he was the primary homicide detective on scene, in a sense, their boss.

Mina and Mrs. Vallinski backed away without me having to ask.

"Jack," Peterson growled out. "Surely you don't think I had anything to do with this. She made donuts, an honest living."

"Donut dough wasn't the only thing she was pressing in the backroom of her donut shop."

Helen dumped the open box of counterfeit bills on the floor as if to drive my point home.

"I didn't know..." He glanced down at her

body. "How am I going to explain this to our mother?"

Either Benny was telling the truth or he deserved an Oscar for best performance from a supporting actor. I dared a glance at Mina and Mrs. Vallinski, caught their accusatory glares on Peterson. Maybe I was being too easy on him.

"Jack." Helen stooped and gathered up a wad of bills. "This doesn't make any sense."

It was as clear as a donut hole to me. "Your dad is a crook, Helen."

"Think, Jack. What were they going to do with all this money? Spend it? They were bound to get caught." She pointed to the wall. "And what's it doing here, in the mayor's mansion, of all places? Why not a warehouse or storage shed?"

I had a hunch. "Davis had a big business deal going down tomorrow night. My guess, a buyer or a fence was going to meet them here and take this inventory off their hands."

Peterson said, "Pretty risky for a mayoral candidate, don't you think?"

"Greed knows no bounds. Hodges was in on it. He and Davis may have rigged the election as well. I bet this shindig was their celebration party."

Helen's face brightened. "That's not it." She rushed to me and knelt at my eye level. "Remember what I told you at the Star Bar? Davis was going to start a smear campaign against my father."

I remembered. "And I told you most people don't pay any attention to those mud-slinging ads."

"That's right." She waved a hand to the stacked boxes. "But who would ignore this?"

"Counterfeit money found in the mayor's mansion. No video to prove it was planted. Pretty convincing evidence against him."

"But it's not that cut and dried," Peterson put in. "The Secret Service takes over counterfeiting cases. They'll sort through the evidence and figure it out. The plot to frame Hodges would have backfired on Davis."

"Davis was too smart for that..." I glanced at Lila, and the answer hit me like a punch to the gut. "He let her think she was the boss, but if anything went wrong, she'd take the fall, and Davis would come out squeaky clean."

"But what was in it for Lila?" Peterson

asked. "She had everything going for her."

I wondered about her motivation too, but thanks to me shooting her dead, we'd never know for sure, so I summed it up for him. "Sometimes everything isn't enough, Benny."

Helen shook the fistful of funny greenbacks at him. "Meanwhile, the scandal over this shit would discredit my dad long enough to knock him out of the race. Long enough for Davis to run unopposed and win by default."

That made sense. Tomorrow night's meeting wasn't about fencing phony bills; it was about getting Hodges busted with the goods. One anonymous call to headquarters, Crime Stoppers, or the Denver Post was all it would take. "But I crashed their party and screwed up their plans."

Peterson got down to business. "Jack, remember that badge I was going to talk to the DA about?"

"You're going to get my job back for me."

"Well, you can forget about that."

"Hey, we made a deal."

"You're suspended indefinitely, until this investigation is complete."

I glanced at the gun and seriously

considered homicide. "Come on, Benny. This case isn't over. Harman is still out there—"

"You killed my sister. That's got to be cleared up. Along with everyone else you killed." He wagged a finger at the corpses lying about.

"Hey, I didn't kill them all."

"That leaves us a lot of sorting out to do then."

"And meanwhile, Harman gets away."

"I'll issue an APB. We'll find him."

"I'll find him, damn it."

"You're going to the hospital. After that, who knows. I may lock you up again just to cut down on my workload."

If I could've gotten up, I would've knocked him down.

***

Paramedics wheeled me out on a gurney.

I felt ridiculous, white sheet draped over a bloody tuxedo jacket. The EMTs had cut off my tux pant leg and popped my kneecap back into place. The second time wasn't any less painful than the first time they'd done it for me at Mrs. Vallinski's. At least this time they'd shot a hypo needle of local anesthetic into my knee. I wished they'd done that before they reset my kneecap. Then they fitted me with a temporary brace around my leg, stiff as a board and fastened with Velcro.

It wasn't hard to predict my future: six weeks in a cast.

Mina strode alongside me, her hand resting on my arm. The gurney stopped at the ambulance back door. Emergency vehicles with a kaleidoscope of flashing lights clogged the driveway: DPD cruisers, two vans marked *CORONER,* and the crime scene investigators' truck. A helicopter thumped overhead, its nightlight sweeping the area. Peterson had called in air support with infrared in hopes of finding Johnny Harman still lurking around the area. Good money had him long gone by now. My Harley stood alone by the *Cableland* sign. I couldn't just leave it there.

I sat up and swiveled my legs out from under the sheet. My left leg stuck out ramrod stiff. "This is where I get off."

Mina glared at me and squeezed my arm. "You're going to the hospital, Jack."

"Later." I pulled my arm free of her grasp.

An EMT stopped me with a hand to my chest. "Detective Peterson's orders."

I sneered at him. "If you ever want to use that hand to wipe your ass again, you'd better move it."

He backed off. "I suppose signing the release form refusing transport to the hospital is out of the question too."

"You got that right." I scooted off the gurney and hobbled toward my bike. "Come on, Mina."

"What?" She gasped. "I'm not dressed to ride a motorcycle."

"Won't we be a sight?"

"Jack." She quick-stepped behind me. "Your leg. You can't ride."

"Sure I can."

"How are you going to shift? You can't bend your knee."

With the help of the pain inoculation and the brace, I pivoted on my bum leg, mounted the bike, and then hefted the Harley upright. "Get on."

"What happened to your rearview mirror?"

"Road rage. Oh. Would you mind knocking back the kickstand for me?"

She did then: "Where are we going?" She climbed on behind me.

"I'm taking you home."

"Are you spending the night?"

"Maybe." I smiled at her over my shoulder.

"I must be crazy, Jack, but I'd like that." She laughed.

I decided not to ruin her mood by telling her the part about me getting a gun and going after Johnny Harman. That was more important than going to the hospital or Peterson's upcoming inquisition.

I fired up the V-Twin.

Mina looped her arms around my waist and pulled her body into my back, warm and secure and full of promise. "Thanks for coming to my rescue, Jack."

"Likewise." I was sure she had no idea what I meant by that. A new love could do a lot for a man's attitude.

Holding the bike up with my right leg, I propped my left foot on the Easy Rider peg, squeezed the clutch, and bumped the shifter down into first gear with my heel.

"Hang on." I released the clutch and weaved between the emergency vehicles to the street. Accelerating down Leetsdale to Colorado Boulevard, I up-shifted with the back of my heel. At Colfax, I swung into the left turn lane and stopped for the red arrow.

This was where it all began, the day I was directing traffic when Maria's Toyota stalled in this very lane. The day I first laid eyes on her, a day that had changed my life. And now, here I was, about to make that same turn, only this time I was a different man, with a different woman, and going a different direction in my life. The feeling was surreal.

The arrow turned green. I accelerated onto Westbound Colfax. Mina hugged me. We had our whole lives ahead of us to see where this relationship might take us. A home in the burbs. Kids and PTA. Disney World and Dinosaur National Park.

Who knew?

Storefront windows reflected us passing by. Mina's yellow shorts and white top revealed lots of exquisite skin. And from this distance, I looked like James Bond in this tux, the blood stains invisible.

Yeah. I didn't need Old Crow to get high.

I slowed for the red light coming up at York. Tires squeaked behind me. An instinctive glance to the left rearview mirror gave me nothing; the glass was gone. I glanced to the right rearview and saw no one, but I heard a car coming up on my left, a black fender gliding up. A black Lincoln fender.

My insides turned to ice. Black Lincolns always came with a shitload trouble.

I twisted the throttle hard, but the transmission was in high gear, making the engine chug. I squeezed the clutch lever and leaned right to switch lanes in an effort to put distance between me and the Lincoln. The sudden maneuver caused my left foot to slip off the highway peg. My heel missed the shifter.

In that instant, the Lincoln pulled up beside me. The passenger window was down. I recognized the driver.

Johnny Harman.

He raised his right arm. The gun in his hand looked big as a howitzer.

Pop. Pop. Pop.

Mina screamed. Her arms loosened around my waist.

"No!"

She slumped over and fell off. I jammed on the brakes, twisted around on the seat in time to see her bounce on the pavement and roll, her arms and legs flopping. Her Nikes flew off her feet.

In that second, the Harley went down on its left side, crashing and screeching and crushing my left leg. My face hit the blacktop, scraped skin and meat and bone. Stars filled my brain. I should've worn a helmet.

Sparks from the skidding bike blew out along both sides of my body until the frame banged to a stop against a light pole.

Lying on my chest, I tried to get up, but the bike pinned my left leg to the pavement. Pushing up with my left elbow, my upper arm bone made a cracking sound and folded in half. My right arm was twisted up under my stomach. I didn't feel anything but a cold wave of shock rippling through my body.

"Mina," I muttered.

I couldn't move, just looked down the road

where her crumpled body lay. *Oh, God, no.*

Tires screeched. Approaching cars stopped. Headlights blazed, making me squint. One car swerved around Mina's body, kept going, probably a drunk, didn't want to be a witness, didn't want to talk to the police.

Somebody help us. Please.

Nobody got out of their cars. Nobody wanted to get involved. Or maybe they were in shock, unsure of what to do. I hoped someone was calling 911 from their cell phone.

My vision began to blur.

Pedestrians rushed to me. One said, "Is he dead?"

Another said, "See if he's got any change on him."

Fucking vultures.

The Lincoln backed up. Stopped. I heard the driver's door open. Shoes appeared. I could see them under the car, walking to the back, around the trunk, then into the street. Harman held the gun at his side and looked down at Mina.

The vultures took flight.

"Hey, mister," a man shouted. He'd gotten out of his car and spoke over the top of his open car door. I could barely see him behind the glare of headlights. "Is she all right?"

Harman raised the gun and fired three times.

Bullets pinged off metal, shattered glass, and thumped into flesh. The man spazzed like he was being electrocuted then dropped to the pavement.

Son of a bitch! Run, everyone, run.

People started screaming. Panicked footsteps retreated. Cars reversed. Tires squealed. Metal crunched. Headlights shrunk back, swung around, and raced away.

Harman stashed his gun and pulled a knife. The blade flashed under the streetlight. He bent over Mina.

His elbow jerked forward.

Her head jerked to the side.

I thought I'd screamed no, but I hadn't made a sound.

Harman stood, knife dripping blood. In the other gloved hand he pinched Mina's eyeball between his thumb and forefinger and held it up to the streetlight as if he was a jeweler admiring a fine diamond.

My blurry vision turned dizzy. I fought to stay conscious, fought to breathe, wished I had a gun and a working hand to use it.

Harman's shoes walked toward me, cool as if taking an afternoon stroll.

My chin seemed one with the asphalt. I couldn't lift my head. I couldn't move.

The shoes stopped in front of my face, deforming in my circus-mirror vision. I could only roll my eyes up to see him stoop down to look at me real close.

"Argghh," was the only sound I could make. Translated it meant, "I'm going to kill your fucking ass."

Harman laughed and held Mina's bloody eyeball in front of my face. Hell had come to earth. Johnny Harman was the devil himself, here to take my soul.

"Ugghh," was the only sound I could force from my throat.

"When are you going to learn, Jack?"

The knife tip glided toward my face, hung in front of my left eye, slowly moving closer. I tried to turn my head away, but I couldn't move. For all I knew I'd broken my neck. The knife blade came closer, so blurry now it looked blunt.

"You can never beat me." He jammed the blade through my lower eyelid, into my eye socket, and up under my eyeball. Pain screamed through my brain like a train wreck. My blurry, dizzied vision doubled: four shoes, two eyeballs. Instead of twisting the blade and cutting my optic muscles and nerves, he held the knife steady as if savoring the moment or thinking about how he could make my suffering worse.

Do it, damnit, cut my eye out. Get it over with!

"But I'm going to give you another chance to try." He yanked out the blade, leaving my eye in the socket, and bent down to where I could see his devilish leer and the tight line of his lips. "Dying is too good for you, Jack. You're going to live in fear of me for the rest of your life. Whenever you look over your shoulder, I'll be there. You may not see me, but I'll see you, and one day, which one you'll never know, I'll finish this fight, and your eye will be staring out from the bottom of a formaldehyde jar, just like all the others."

"Hughhhh." *I'll hunt you down like a dog, motherfucker.*

The shoes walked away.

I felt faint.

A car door slammed. The Lincoln roared out of view.

And then nothing.

Chapter Twenty-Eight

WHISKEY HEAVEN was a tranquil place where anything was possible. I was healed. I didn't walk with a limp from a bum left leg, and I didn't have a six-month-old scar under my left eye. In my drunken state, I sat up straight and proud on my Harley, the wind in my hair and a woman's arms around my waist, snuggled up close like she belonged to me. Sometimes in this heaven of mine, she was Maria, her memory as vivid as if she were still alive. Sometimes she was Mina Finetree, a ghostly figure of a love that could have been but never was.

And since I believed in heaven, I also believed in hell. On some of my worst benders, the devil rode behind me, snuggled up close like I belonged to him.

"Hey, Jack," a deep voice said.

His sinewy red arms wrapped around my waist, fingers interlaced, fingers with the shape and sheen of knife blades. The fire he breathed down the back of my neck chilled me to the bone.

Whiskey hell was no place for pussies.

"Jack."

A stolen glance to the rearview mirror shook me with a start. Canted eyes leered over my shoulder. His eyebrows were made of fire that seared his face red, and lizard-like skin stretched over high cheek bones that framed a hooked nose. Oh, he tried to disguise himself, all right, but he couldn't fool me. Johnny Harman was the devil looking over my shoulder.

"You're a loser, Jack."

The V-Twin rumbled and roared. Johnny Harman shook my shoulders, shook the bike, tipped it left and right, back and forth, tires skidding and rubber smoking.

"Stop it!" I shouted. "Leave me alone!"

"Jack."

The bike went down, skidding and crashing as some external force pried into my drunken stupor. The pavement raced up to my face. Whiskey hell exploded. I opened my eyes. Blinked dirt. I'd awoke face-down in the dirt. Under a bridge. Where I belonged. I gasped. Bile rushed up the back of my throat, hot and salty, and spewed out my mouth, a gicky yellow puke. Nothing new for Jack Sabre. It happened every time I crashed back to reality like this.

I spit and fell back into whiskey's dark embrace.

A rhythmic beeping greeted my next conscious moment. I knew I was alive because I could taste my tongue, dry as Bigfoot's shoe leather. My eyelids felt glued shut, all sticky from gloppy tears, but I could tell I was lying on my back, not face down in the dirt, as usual. My head lay on a pillow, better than a rock or a Larimer Street curb. I inhaled hospital air. It had that distinctive tang to it. At least I wasn't waking up in the drunk-tank this time.

"Jack." An angel's voice. "I know you're awake."

Oh crap.

Not an angel but Mamma Helen Hodges. Her voice sounded terse, locked and loaded for another rant about my drinking. About me throwing my life away. My career. I didn't want to hear it again.

"You really hit bottom this time, Jack. The sewer. The pits."

But I was going to hear it anyway. *Blah, blah, blah.*

"They found you under the Speer Boulevard Bridge."

They? They who? I should kill them for fucking up my pity party.

I sensed her leaning over me, the creak of the bed rail, the weight of her shadow on my face.

"How many days have you been sober in the last six months?"

None, I hoped.

"I can count them on one hand, the day before, the day of, and the day after Mina's funeral."

A noose lynched my heart, strung it up in my throat, and let it sway in a prickly wind of despair. Only six months since her funeral? Six centuries wouldn't have been long enough. What difference did it make? Dead was dead forever.

"I know you can hear me, Jack."

I ignored her.

The bed motor whined, angled me up to a

sitting position. She was as hard to ignore as an oncoming locomotive.

"Open your eyes."

I exaggerated a sigh, blinked my eyes open, and allowed reality to rush in on me. I wasn't wearing a shirt. Wires were taped to my chest and connected to that beeping machine. A white sheet lay folded back across my lap. Next to me, a bed table on coasters held a silver dome-covered dish and a plastic cup with a sippy straw.

I glanced at Helen. Not a blond hair out of place, stiff pantsuit and blazer, boring beige. She'd pinned a gold brooch to the lapel. Her smile seemed more perturbed than friendly. "Welcome back, Jack."

"I need a drink," I rasped out, my voice dry and throaty.

She handed me the sippy cup. An IV needle protruded from the back of my right hand. The plastic tube led to a bag hanging on a chrome hook, half full of a clear liquid. I wished it was grain alcohol.

I sucked cool water through the straw and eyed the covered dish. My stomach rolled a little, telling me it was hungry.

Helen swiveled the bed tray up to me. "Eat."

I peeked under the dish's lid: scrambled eggs, bacon, tater tots and toast, then set the lid aside. "At least I didn't miss breakfast."

"You've already missed one, Jack."

I'd been here for two days? How the hell did I pee? I lifted the white sheet. Sure enough. I was wearing *Depends.*

Fuck. I'd been pissing in diapers for two days.

"Did you see what they put on me here?" I hoped not.

"You make your own misery, Jack."

I dropped the sheet and swallowed my pride, what little I had left. Besides, how much pride did it take to pass out drunk and naked under a bridge? Guess I finally got the memo. Porky was right about me. I'd taken Danny's place on the skids.

The beeping machine irritated the piss out of me. I dug into my breakfast.

She got on her cell phone. "He's awake."

Mrs. Vallinski walked in wearing a flowery dress as if it were springtime in the Rockies.

Oh, it was.

She smiled at me, that motherly kind of nonjudgmental smile that I needed. "Good morning, Jack." She set a Walmart sack on the end of my bed.

Mouth full of food, I nodded to her.

Helen closed her phone. "He's on his way," she said to Mrs. Vallinski.

"Who?" I mumbled.

"Just eat."

Mrs. V. started unloading the sack. "New jeans, shirt, shoes." She held up a package of Speedo looking underpants and whistled. "Socks. New wallet. Belt." She showed me a small box, opened it, the top on a hinge. "Nice watch. Oh I know it looks expensive, but it was only nine bucks on sale."

A nine-dollar watch. I'd hit the jackpot. But all their fuss was for nothing. I'd be out of here soon, back under a bridge, getting friendly again with my old friend Old Crow.

Finished with my meal, I scooted the tray aside. For the first time in a long time I actually felt like I wanted to live.

Helen patted my arm. "My dad still wants

to see you, Jack, about your Distinguished Service Cross, remember? You saved his ass."

Mayor Hodges. *Beware the company you keep.* That was the advice I'd given him. From a similar hospital bed. After that night. After Mina's death...

I shook the memory from my head. "He can stick his stupid medal up his ass." Besides, I wasn't officially on the force that night.

The mayor was cleared of having any part in the counterfeit money business, but he wouldn't get any medals from me for being a good father. When the shit came down, he just stood there like a wart on a toad and did nothing to help Helen or me.

But he did call 9-1-1, first chance he got after the shooting had started, so I'd give him credit for that.

Benny Peterson strode into the room wearing that same K-Mart suit and striped tie. He carried a satchel and a grim look on his brow.

Mrs. Vallinski wheeled the bed table back out of the way, and then quick-stepped to Helen at the foot of my bed. Their expressions matched Peterson's: concerned.

I smelled trouble. With my luck I'd be

going back to the slammer for indecent exposure. "What's up?"

Peterson approached my bedside. "I brought you something." He set the satchel on the bed.

"I'll bet it's not a bottle of booze."

"Better." He opened the satchel and pulled out a brown paper bag.

That got my interest.

"The Shoot Team has cleared you of any wrong doing, and the DA decided you acted in self defense when you killed Vallinski."

"How nice of them to be on my side for a change. And you? What about your sister? I shot her in the fuckin' heart. You forgive me for that?"

"I'm working on it." He opened the sack and peered inside. "But some things have to be put aside for more important matters."

He dumped the contents in my lap: keys with Ford logos on the black thumb pads. A laminated ID card. A gold badge...number *121848*. My number. My badge. The stuff I'd turned over to Captain Salvador. My breath hitched.

"It's time to go back to work, Jack."

I sat up straight. "Oh, no. Get this shit out

of here."

"This represents who you are, Jack Sabre. Not a bottle of booze. Not the Star Bar. Not the drunk tank. *You* are a cop. *We* are partners."

"Yeah? How well did that work out for you?"

"Look, Jack. You'll have to clear medical and get the okay from the department shrink before you can carry a gun, but I'm not willing to give up on you. Neither are Helen and Mrs. Vallinski. So don't give up on yourself."

"I already have, besides..." I rubbed my whisker-bristled chin. "Drinking is hard work. I've already got a full-time job."

"So that's a no?"

"Hey, Benny. You catch on real fast. Leave me the fuck alone."

He held his breath and looked at me like I'd said something stupid. I gave him an I-dare-you-to-say-anything glare. If I weren't wearing diapers I'd have jumped out of bed and kicked his ass.

Partner, hell.

He exhaled and rolled the bed table in front of me.

"What now?"

Staring at me, he pulled a folder from his satchel and opened it like it was a hymnal.

I frowned at him. "Show and tell?"

He selected a paper and laid it on the bed table where I could see it real good.

I looked down, expecting a court summons for drunk and disorderly, but saw a photograph, a crime scene photo of a woman lying on a tile floor, a kitchen floor maybe. She lay on her side, wore a green tank top and white shorts. Her legs were thrown askew, her arms spread, one forward and one back. A mop of brown hair concealed her face.

Peterson said, "Meet Claire Benson."

I didn't know any Claire Benson. DPD homicide wouldn't need to question me about her. Unless... My heart lurched. Unless I got so drunk I'd done something to her. Peterson couldn't possibly think I'd killed her. "Why are you showing me this?"

He laid out another photo: Claire's face from a different angle. Her left eye had been gouged out, the black socket clearly visible.

My insides turned over. I looked up at Benny. "He's back."

"Not a sign of him in six months." Benny

set down another photo: another angle of the body, this one with the wall behind her visible. A playing card had been pinned to the wall: a Jack of Spades.

"Black Jack," I muttered.

"He left you a message."

The irony of the one-eyed Jack hadn't escaped me, like he was predicting my future vision problems.

My heart jack-hammered against my ribs. "So Johnny Harman wants to play games with me at the expense of innocent women." He had to know it would piss me off enough to put me in the fight.

Peterson poked his finger at the top picture. "Help us get this guy, Jack."

Helen looked at me expectantly. Mrs. Vallinski nodded. My angels at the ready.

I picked up my badge and clenched it in my fist, the black cloud of murder on my mind. "I'm in."

About the Author

There's nothing mundane in the writing world of **Terry Wright**. Tension, conflict, and suspense propel his readers through the pages as if they were on fire. Published in Science Fiction, Supernatural, and Horror, his mastery of the action thriller has also won him International acclaim as an accomplished screenplay writer. A longtime member of the Rocky Mountain Fiction Writers, he has served on their board of directors, and for five years, he ran their annual Colorado Gold Writing Contest. He is also the editor and owner of TWB Press. Terry lives near Denver with his wife, Bobette, and their Yorkie named Taz.

http://www.twbpress.com

Terry Wright